ARENA LIGHTS

FU FIRE HOCKEY SERIES

MANDI BECK

Arena Lights

Copyright 2019 by Mandi Beck

Cover Designer: Letitia Hasser, RBA Designs

Cover Photo: Lauren Perry, Perrywinkle Photography

Copy Editor: Jenny Simms, Edits 4 Indies

To my Hockey Boy,
you'll always be my favorite player.
And to Ran,
thank you for allowing us to dream our dreams and doing your best
to make them come true.

ALSO BY MANDI BECK

FU Hockey Series

Sin Bin

Arena Lights

Sweater Weather

Caged Love

Love Hurts

Love Burns

Wrecked Series

Stoned

Rhythm

Sugar

Cherry Falls Series

1228 Wanderlust Lane

1026 Wild Way

Standalone

Twisted

This is your moment. You're meant to be here. -Herb Brooks

1

MAEVE

"**A**re you even listening to me?"

I pop my head out of the closet at my sister's question. I was not listening to her, and she busted me. In my defense, she hasn't stopped talking since she barged into my room twenty minutes ago and threw herself on my bed right in the middle of the clothes I had laid out to pack.

"Sorry, Millie, what did you say?"

Sighing in exasperation, her breath ruffling her red hair the exact shade of mine, she repeats herself. "Two weeks away without our brother or daddy! Can you say party? Because I can. I can also say sex. And party, and drinking, and sex," my twin goes on excitedly. I'm just as excited about this trip, but just for different reasons.

"You may have mentioned a couple of those more than once. I'm not sure if you said sex yet. Did you say sex? I wasn't really paying attention." All I can do is laugh. Millie acts like we lead a wicked sheltered life. Just because our older brother, the captain of the hockey team, has eyes and ears all over campus —making it a little harder to date—and our dad just happens to be the coach of our softball team—and therefore always around—doesn't mean we don't get a chance to do all the things she's talking about. Not that I do, because there is more to being in college than invites to frat parties, drinking, and hooking up. Even if Millie doesn't think so.

"Aren't you even a little excited? No hockey boys around to go back to Levi and snitch about every move we make?"

I'm just about to answer when a voice comes from the doorway. "What moves you making, Mill?"

"Levi!" she squeaks, jumping from the bed. "Don't sneak up on us. We're having a private conversation." She practically hisses at our older brother. His wide shoulders fill the doorway, as he stands leaning against the doorframe with his arms crossed over his broad chest. She knows she's been caught.

"I can tell." Levi looks over at me. "How about you, Maevey? Are you making moves?" he asks, knowing damn well he'll get more out of me than Millie. She knows it too, which is why she doesn't give me a chance to answer.

"Nobody is making any moves. We're just packing for Arizona. What do you want?" Millie hurries to say, the flush on her face making the freckles sprinkled across her nose more prominent.

"Just coming to drop clothes off and to tell you that my favorite roommate is going with you guys on your little trip," he says smugly. Obviously, he heard Millie's little "no hockey boys" dig.

"What? Who? It's not a hockey trip; it's a softball and base-ball trip!" she whines.

Trying to defuse the situation before she throws a *real* hissy, I say, "Oh, calm down, Millie. He's joking."

"Umm, no, I'm not."

Confused myself now, I ask, "You're not? Millie's right; it's a softball and baseball clinic. Why would a hockey player be going? And who is your favorite roommate? You have three."

"Well, Benny is my favorite today. Mostly because he's

tagging along to make sure there aren't any moves being made."
He shoots a smug look at Millie, throwing her words back at
her. "His sister is your assistant coach and in charge of the
whole trip since Dad isn't going. Plus, their family lives in
Arizona, so she asked if Benny could come with them. This
way, they can visit their parents, and he can be a chaperone,
cutting the team's costs. It just makes the most sense."

Levi looks way too pleased about this, and Millie looks
about to cry. I swear that boy loves making her life hell. Well,
hell as far as Mill is concerned anyway.

"So not fair!" She huffs and stomps from my room, calling
for Mom like she can put a stop to this.

"She's maaaaaaddd," he gloats.

"You knew she would be. That's why you came all the way
over here to tell us." He's not fooling me.

"It's true."

"You're shameless." My brother flashes his stupid dimples at
me. "Those don't work on me like they do all your little girl-
friends or Mom." He just smiles wider and walks out of the
room whistling. With a shake of my head, I go back to packing.
I don't care if Benny Hayes is going on the trip. I'm not going to
party it up. It's a great clinic, and one I've been excited for. Our
university has one of the best softball teams in the country.
We've had a rough preseason, though, with losing our star
pitcher, which is why my dad isn't going along. He's scouting
for a new starter to take Stella's place. We have other pitchers;
we just don't have another Stella. We need this clinic not only
for a morale boost, but to get our asses ready to defend our title
in the upcoming season as well. Benny can do whatever the
hell he wants because I'll be playing softball. Millie will just
have to party it up some other time, though I can't even say I'm
upset about that. At least now, he'll be babysitting her, and I
won't have to worry about her as much.

Once I'm finally packed, I make my way downstairs. My

mom calls out, and I follow their voices into the dining room where they all sit at the table for dinner. My mom stands firm on the rule of if we're all in the house, we're all sitting for dinner together as a family no matter what. Millie still complains about her ruined trip, and Levi still loves it. "Mom, it's not even fair." My sister huffs as she pushes her chicken around her plate petulantly.

"What isn't fair, Mill? Why does it even matter to you? Maeve doesn't mind." Levi is the poster boy for innocence right now with his tossed dirty blond hair, dimpled grin, and his stupidly perfect white teeth.

"Oh, cut the crap. You and your dumb hockey boys are always hovering. And why are you sitting in Dad's chair? You're not the boss of anything." My mom shakes her head at the two of them as I do my best not to laugh. I haven't seen Millie this upset in a long time. She must have had some big plans for this trip. I don't know when she thinks we'll have time for all her extracurricular activity; it's a jam-packed schedule of softball games and clinics.

"I'm the man of the house when Dad isn't home, which kinda does make me the boss of shit."

"Language, Levi," warns our mother. "And no, you're not the boss. I am. Even when Daddy *is* here, and don't any of you forget it." Truer words were never spoken. "Tell your friend to leave your sisters be. They don't need a keeper. They're good girls."

Millie harrumphs at Levi smugly.

"They're good girls because of us *keeping*, Ma. And Because Maeve is kind of boring."

"Hey!" I admonish.

"It's true, you are," Millie chimes in.

"Oh, now you're on his side?"

My sister just shrugs. "Well, maybe not boring, but definitely not as fun as me." She tries to soothe. The traitor.

Mom smiles at me, patting my hand. She knows how these two are. Two of a kind really. More so than Millie and me, and we're twins. My brother and I may be thick as thieves, but those two might as well be the same person.

"Anyway, you act like I put Benny up to this or have any control," Levi insists. "It's his sister's responsibility, and she wants him along. Not my deal." He shovels more food into his mouth, trying to appear all innocent. It may not have been his idea for Benny to go on the trip, but it sure as hell was his idea for him to keep an eye on us.

"Well, regardless if it was your idea or not, tell your little friend we don't need a babysitter. I already have Maeve. She keeps us both out of trouble." Millie points her fork at him. "I mean it. I won't do any of your laundry for a month! You won't be such a lady-killer when you smell like ass," she warns.

"Maevey does my laundry. Nice try, though, short stack," he shoots back, knowing he has her there.

"Okay, you three, that's enough. Maeve, Millie, just watch out for each other and stay out of trouble. If you do that, it won't matter a bit that Benny is there. He'll probably be off visiting his parents or something anyway," my mother, always the referee and voice of reason, says calmly. Although I'm sure he won't be doing anything so wholesome. Still, I can tell by the crestfallen look on Millie's face that it doesn't appease her. She just sees all her fun swirling down the drain in front of her like soap after a shower.

Outside McKenzie Hall where the softball training facility along with the sophomore dorms are located, we wait to board the buses that will take us to the airport. Out of the frigid cold and on our way to the sun and fun in Arizona. Some of the girls dressed for the Arizona temps instead of the cold Boston morning, Millie being one of them.

"I'm freezing, sissy. Keep me warm." She's practically crawling under my hoodie right now to find warmth.

"Why didn't you wear clothes?"

"I did!" My sister's clad in a pair of booty shorts, Vans without socks, of course, and a cute little shirt that hangs off one shoulder. Keyword being little.

"You did not! It's December in Boston, Millie. We're not in Phoenix yet." Even as I say it, I'm peeling off my hoodie to give to her. If she gets sick, I'll just have to take care of her, and I want to be able to focus on softball, not my sicky poo pain sister. At least I have a long-sleeve shirt on underneath to keep me warm-ish.

"Oh, thank you, thank you, thank you!" Her teeth chatter as she slips it over her head, careful not to mess her carefully done up hair.

"You do realize we're going right to the hotel before we head to orientation, right? You could have just dressed comfortably in warm clothes and got ready at the hotel."

"You should never travel in something you wouldn't go out in. Like *out* out, not to Walmart *out*," she shoots back, looking at my comfy black leggings, long-sleeve FU FIRE shirt, and gym shoes in disdain.

"Ummm...I would wear this *out* out, and I was nice and warm. Unlike someone else I know." My pointed look is ignored.

"She has a point, Mill," our friend and catcher, Kenna, says as she shoulder bumps my sister. "We know you're hot. You don't have to impress us with those long ass legs."

We're joined by a couple more of our friends just as Coach Hayes comes out of the building with Benny right behind her. "Oh my, god. Please tell me that Benny Hayes is coming on this trip with us," Lakyn practically purrs.

"Ugh, don't get me started!" Millie huffs, turning her back on the pair as if that would make Benny disappear.

Kenna's eyes bug comically. "Why are we upset about this? He's so freaking hot." He really is.

"He's a hockey boy. Just put on the planet to drive me nuts and snitch to my brother about everything."

I can't help but laugh because she's so damn dramatic. "Millie, he's not gonna snitch on you for anything." She's *really* bent about this. "He's probably not even going to be around that much. Levi said he was going with to visit his parents."

"And to *chaperone.*"

"He can chaperone the hell out of me," Lakyn volunteers.

"Right?" Kenna agrees. "I don't get why you wouldn't want some hottie hanging around."

"He's a hockey boy!" Millie says as if that explains everything. She's met with blank stares and slow blinks. "Fine. You guys keep him occupied while I find someone who doesn't live with my brother to hook up with. Baseball butts are way more my style anyway."

Before any of us have a chance to comment, Coach Hayes blows her whistle to get our attention. She's flanked by Benny on one side and one of the athletic department's physical therapists, Hannah, on the other.

"Morning, ladies! Let's load up and head out of here. The baseball team will be on a bus behind us. If at any time during our trip you should need something, have an issue, a question, whatever, you can come find me or one of our chaperones, Hannah Carney or Benny Hayes." Hannah smiles and gives a little wave. Benny just lifts his chin, his eyes barely visible under the brim of his baseball cap as he stands, legs spread, sweats hanging on his hips, hands buried in the front pocket of his hoodie. Basically, the college athlete uniform complete with resting jock face, which is the same as resting bitch face, only with a penis. I try not to notice how good looking he really is, but it's impossible. I've never paid too much attention because I've never spent any time around him without my brother.

At Benny's greeting, if you can call it that, a collective squeal ripples over the group of girls. I'm not even sure why, but it startles me. It's the same reaction my brother gets all over campus —did all through high school too, actually—so you'd think I'd be used to it by now. Coach shakes her head because clearly, she's not used to it either. "I expect you all to be on your best behavior. We will be in Arizona representing not only Fulton University but also Coach Sexton. We are to conduct ourselves as if he were there. I have every faith that we will make him proud both on and off the field while we're away." Her gaze touches over our group. Satisfied that we hear the message loud and clear, she nods, then waves her hand for us to file onto the bus. Let the fun begin.

2

BENNY

Two weeks in Arizona with fifteen hot ass softball players doesn't sound like a bad way to spend the last half of my winter break. Plus, it will be great to see my parents. I didn't go home over Christmas because I didn't want to take off work for this trip and an additional one. I don't work a ton of hours as it is, and the campus Pro Shop is a sweet gig.

With my sister tapping away at her phone, leaving me to my own devices as she makes sure everything is set for our arrival, I kick back and let my gaze roam over all the softball players scattered around the gate. As a chaperone I shouldn't be wondering which ones I can hook up with up on this little trip, but I am. Not that I don't have plenty of chicks to hit up once I'm back in Phoenix, but this just gives me something to do while I wait for our flight to board. Kenna and Lakyn I know for a fact will let me smash. My eyes flick over a couple of the girls I've already hooked up with. I don't go back for seconds if I can help it. It just gives them the wrong idea, and I'm not about that boyfriend life. The Sexton twins are sitting together, as usual. They're never apart. It's a shame that they're off-limits because I would give them a double ride all day long. They're identical, both with flaming red hair, hazel eyes, and covered in freckles that shouldn't be sexy but are. Long ass legs and a perfect handful of tits. But again, totally off-limits. In fact, that's their nickname and what everyone in the house calls them. Their brother is not only the captain of our hockey team but also my roommate, so that makes them *off-limits* on every level. I'm not trying to get my fucking ass kicked by Levi. It really is too fucking bad. I bet Millie would be wild as fuck. She's the *bad* twin out of the two. Their brother always has someone on campus keeping an eye out, and it's always her getting them into trouble. Maeve is super chill. She balances the two out for sure. Maybe she's the real freak. You know what they say about the quiet ones. I'm not going to be the one who finds out, though. I was warned by their brother already to keep my distance but to also make sure that nobody else goes near them while they're in Arizona. They're my responsibility since he had to stay back. Anything happens to them, and I'm fucked. He takes his sisters as seriously as he takes hockey, and he takes that shit as seriously as I do.

Finally, before I can think any more about the twins and how that's never gonna happen, our flight is announced, and everyone starts gathering their things and lining up. I grab my sister's bag and hold my hand out to help her out of her chair. She takes it and smiles. "Thanks, little brother. Sorry we didn't get seats together. You waited too long to make up your mind."

Olivia takes the little suitcase from me. "No worries. I'm a big boy. I'm sure I can find my way without having to sit next to my big sister," I tease.

"As long as you make it onto the plane and stay out of the mile-high club, I'll consider it a win." Her stern look has me laughing as much as the mile-high club dig did.

"Mile-high club? Is that what you old folks call it? Us young kids just call it fu—" My sister claps a hand over my mouth.

"Don't you dare. I don't care what you call it. Don't do it."
With a pat to my cheek, she moves to stand in line, leaving me
to follow. I let Lakyn and a couple of the other girls go before
me. Not because I'm a gentleman but because it will give me an
ass to stare at that doesn't belong to my sister as we make our
way to our seats. I don't know who I'm sitting with, only that I'm
on an aisle and the emergency row so I can have some leg room
for my six-foot-four self. *8C, 9C, 10C, here I am.* There isn't
anyone else in the row yet, so maybe I'll get lucky and have the
whole thing to myself.

"I can't believe they put the baseball team on a different
flight. That's so lame."

"I know, right?"

I don't look up as the girls go on talking about how unfair
shit is, just continue scrolling on my phone through my
playlists looking for something to listen to and drown them out.

"They better not have them at different hotels too. That
would suck so bad. I mean, it's not like any of us will have cars. I
guess we can Uber to wherever they're staying."

Why the hell do they care where the guys are staying? It's
not like they won't be exactly where the girls are. The whole
fucking time.

"Or they can Uber to us, but then we can't just leave if we
want to."

I'm turned around, trying to see who the two girls are when
I feel someone standing beside me in the aisle.

"Can I get by, please?"

My gaze travels up long legs, over slim thighs with just the
tiniest gap and a pinched waist, up, up, up until I land on a
sweet rack covered by a gray Fulton University shirt and a long
red braid draped over the shoulder...shit. One last lingering
look at the fucking hot curves in front of me, and I sigh at the
irony.

Once Maeve settles in the middle seat, an older guy having

already occupied the window seat, she turns to me. "Gum?" I watch as she pops a piece in her mouth, her full pink lips closing around the stick. Damn.

"Thanks, Maeve." I take the piece from her and tell myself not to check her out again for the rest of the flight. Shouldn't be hard. *I* shouldn't be hard. Fuck. It must be the lack of sleep. With a tug on my hat, I bring the brim low over my eyes and slouch down in my seat as far as I can comfortably. It's impossible. With a sigh, I straighten again.

"Here." She hands me one of those neck pillow things. "This should help."

"What are you going to use?" I feel bad taking it from her.

"I'll be fine. I can't sleep on planes anyway. I brought it because Millie falls asleep before takeoff and ends up lying on me. If I pack the pillow, she stays upright. But since she's not my problem on this flight, you can use it." She smiles.

"So what you're saying is you don't want me all up in your personal space so I should use the pillow."

"Basically. I don't want to have to embarrass you when you drool all over my shoulder or cop a feel in your sleep. That would seriously ruin all my brother's plans of you chaperoning, and it'd be wicked hard to explain to him. I mean, you can try, but do you really want to?"

Maeve Sexton is funny. Who knew?

"I'd make you do it. He'd hit me first and ask questions later." That's no lie.

"Oh, he'd hit you first regardless." She smiles, revealing a dimple in her cheek.

Without thinking, I stick my finger in it. "Cute."

"Ow." She laughs and rubs the spot on her face that I just assaulted. My fingers are blunt, my hands beat up from hockey. I should have gone in a little softer. Hell, I shouldn't have gone in at all.

"My bad. I forget that they're like caveman hands. At least they don't smell."

With a wrinkled nose, she agrees, "So true! Levi loves to smother us with his stinky hockey hands all the time."

"It's a sign of affection."

"Well, you guys can keep that shit to yourself. Love me less," Maeve says sternly with a wrinkle of her nose, making me laugh.

"I thought your sister was the dramatic one?"

"Oh, she is. She so is. She wouldn't even be talking to you right now if she were in my seat. She's wicked pissed you're on this trip."

"What? Why?" I ask just as they're starting the preflight check.

"She has big plans for this weekend and doesn't want any hockey boys around." Maeve shrugs. "She's our little drama llama."

"Fuck, I guess. You know I'm gonna be all up in her shit now right?" I rub my hands together. "This will be so fun." My smile is wicked. It really will be fun. What in the hell does Millie Sexton want to get into that she doesn't want her brother to know about?

A low groan rumbles from next to me. "You know you'll be torturing me too, right?"

"Not my problem. She's your drama llama, not mine."

Her pointy little elbow connects with my ribs. "You're just mean. I will get even, though. I promise."

Craning my neck, I look over the seat, and my gaze collides with a beady-eyed glare from Millie. "Holy shit, you weren't lying. She really does hate me."

Maeve nods. "This is not me being dramatic. It's the gospel. Good thing she can't push you out of the plane because she might try."

With a shake of my head, I pull the pink and gray striped

pillow around my neck, unable to fasten it at the front because it's clearly made for little necks. "So why are you sitting over here instead of with your girls?"

The plane starts taxiing from the gate, gathering speed, and I watch as Maeve checks her seat belt once, twice, three times. Is she nervous? My question is answered when she white-knuckle grips the armrest between us as the plane ascends. I nudge her foot with mine. "You didn't answer my question. How'd I get you and your fluffy pillow?" Maybe talking will distract her.

She takes a breath. "I booked at a different time. Wasn't sure I was going to make it because of a class I was trying to get into." It's said quickly, her lips rolled in and pressed between her teeth the moment the words leave her mouth. I'm trying to think of another question to ask when the plane does a little dip and shimmy, making Maeve jump and latch onto my arm, her nails biting into my skin even through my hoodie. Her eyes are screwed closed, head pressed into the back of her seat. She looks half a second away from a panic attack. The plane levels, and Maeve slowly begins to relax next to me.

"You good?"

"Yeah, sorry. I hate takeoff. The rest of the flight doesn't bother me, just the takeoff. I'm always expecting the plane to burst into flames before we even get into the air." She laughs nervously.

"Ummm...you sure you're not the drama queen?" Her level of drama is kind of cute. But I've seen firsthand how cute can turn to not so cute with a flip of a switch.

"I'm a girl, so I'm moderately dramatic through genetics. It can't be helped. Just as boys are born with the asshole gene, girls are born with the drama gene." She shrugs, smothering a little grin. "It's science."

With a look that clearly says how crazy I think she is, I can't help but laugh. "I'm pretty sure that's not how science works."

"Are you a science major?"

"No."

"Then you don't know shit," Maeve says matter-of-factly and sticks her tongue out at me before turning her attention to the book she pulls from her bag. A science book. A science book on...genetics.

"They teach you that in your fancy book? You might need to do some more research."

"No. I learned that from having an older brother and constantly being around all his friends all my life. It's like a life-long experiment at this point."

"So you're saying I'm an asshole?" I'm slightly offended.

"Not that you're an asshole but that you have the ability to be one just as I have the ability to be dramatic."

"And you don't think that *that's* a little dramatic?"

She shrugs. "Maybe it is, maybe it isn't, but since you're my brother's friend, I guess we'll never know. I'll have to do my research on someone else."

It's all said jokingly. She's not even a little serious about any of it, and still, it makes me want to fight an imaginary, maybe asshole who Maeve would give her attention to. Even if she wasn't Levi's sister, I don't mess around with sweet girls like her because she's right, I am an asshole. Just like her brother and the rest of his friends she's been surrounded by all her life. We're all just in it for the smash and dash. And *that* makes me all kinds of an asshole, one who has no business even talking to hot as fuck Maeve Sexton. Fuck me, this is going to be the longest flight and even longer two weeks of my life.

3

MAEVE

"What were you doing being all nicey-nice to Benny Hayes?" Millie asks as we unpack our suitcases. We've been at the hotel for all of five minutes, and she's already grilling me. I'm actually surprised she waited this long, considering she gave me the stink eye on the whole bus ride from the airport.

"I wasn't being all anything. We were just talking." I hang up the couple of sundresses I brought on my side of the closet. The rooms are huge, complete with a kitchenette area so that we can cook some food instead of always eating on campus. We would typically stay in the dorms for this clinic, but a recent fire has them out of commission. The hotel is literally right across the street, though, so we can walk over to the cafeteria and the fields. "Did you want me to ignore him the whole flight?" There's no way I could have, even if I tried. He's too much...just too much everything for that. Not only his size, which is pretty damn impressive up close, but Benny has a presence about him without even trying. I loved joking around with him, and our banter was easy. Maybe because he was *safe* just by being Levi's friend. I could relax and be me because I knew nothing could come of it.

"No, but you were all cozy, and you gave him my pillow!"

"It's my pillow, Mill, and we were definitely *not* cozy." Making my way into the bathroom, I strip off my leggings and shirt so I can shower really quick before we go to our team meeting. "We sat together, we chatted a bit, then he went to sleep. The end." I won't mention how even with the borrowed pillow, he ended up leaned against me. Or that I liked it. And I especially won't divulge that the clean smell of his cologne clinging to me is the real reason I need to shower.

Millie comes into the bathroom, not caring that I'm in the shower. "Well, you shouldn't be nice to him. He'll get ideas and want to hang around, and I do *not* want him hanging around, Maeve." She whips the curtain back, and I do my best to cover my bits.

"Seriously, Mill?" My sister has no boundaries with anyone, but especially not with me.

She pulls the curtain closed again. "I'm serious, Maeve. There are a whole bunch of baseball teams here, and we can find soooo many boys to keep us occupied while we're here." Her tone is positively wistful.

"You know there isn't going to be a whole lot of time for all that, right?"

"There's always time for boys." She pokes her head around the curtain. "So don't like him, okay, sissy?" Oh, she's really pouring on the sugar now. That's the only time the *sissy* card gets pulled.

I flick water at her, and she retreats. "I don't like him. I don't even know him. Plus, he's Levi's roommate." That in and of itself makes the argument moot. Even if I did like him, which I don't—at least, I don't think—my brother would never let it fly. He's never bothered too much with any of my relationships.

Mostly because they've all been short lived or kept quiet, but also, they weren't with anyone in his circle. Benny is totally in Levi's orbit. He's his roommate *and* teammate, which makes them part of the hockey boy brotherhood or whatever they are. Millie is a totally different story. She always goes for the bad boys, which is what makes Levi get all up in her business.

"Yeah, you're right. That's a big one. Levi would kick his ass." Obviously satisfied with that, she leaves, calling back, "Hurry up. We have to be there in twenty-five minutes. This is why I came prepared."

"Liar! You came dressed for summer because you thought you might get to sit next to some Hottie McHotterson," I shout over the sound of the water falling around me and the whir of the exhaust fan. "And don't pretend you don't hear me," I add for good measure, positive that I'm right.

"Are you sure that isn't mine?" Millie asks for the third time, pointing at my romper. It was one of the new ones I had bought just for this trip and super cute with its pink and white arrows all over the gray cotton.

"I'm positive. Nice try, though," I volley as I stand to throw my plate away. After the meeting, we were able to grab an early dinner at the cafeteria and get a quick tour of the fields and campus, apart from the dorms that were in the process of being gutted and rebuilt. "And no, you may not borrow it. I'll never see it again. Just like I've never seen that Adidas track suit you promised to hang right back up in my closet."

My sister pretends she doesn't hear me and links her arm with mine, knowing damn well that I'm right. "Are you coming with us over to Fraternity Village tomorrow night? We were invited by a couple of the baseballers."

"You know that the sisters are not going to like that." Sorority girls can be a little territorial, so they will not appreciate us being there.

"We were invited. Plus, it's winter break for them, which is weird to say since it's so hot. I'm sure most aren't even on campus. And you know what that means?" she singsongs.

"Ummm...no." I laugh at her exasperated expression.

"It means more boys for us." Ever the boy crazy twin, I should have known she was going there.

"Where are there more boys?" Lakyn asks as she and Kenna join us at the crosswalk leading back to our hotel.

"I was telling Maeve about the party tomorrow night."

"Yes, girl! You are totally going, Maeve."

"You guys act like I never do anything fun with you. I'm fun." My friends and sister are going to give me a complex.

"You are fun!" Kenna is hurried to assure me, her smile just as quick as her words.

"But you're also the responsible one, and the DD whenever we go anywhere," Lakyn adds, hooking my other arm. My pale, freckle-covered skin a stark contrast to her tanned, olive, and freckle-free one.

"Not that we aren't grateful for that! You've saved my ass more times than I can count," my sister offers unnecessarily. I know just how many times I've come to her rescue, and it's more times than she even realizes. She keeps me on my toes, that's for sure. Her hazel eyes twinkle, the same mossy color except for the blue bursts in mine.

"I'm sure I'll go, depending on what happens on the field tomorrow. What are we doing tonight, though?" It's too early to go sit in the hotel room, but we've just eaten, and we aren't old enough for any of the bars that I saw on the ride in.

"I think there was a coffee shop around the block from us," Kenna offers as a suggestion.

"I could totally go for some coffee. What time is curfew?" They won't care, but I'm not blowing curfew our first night here, especially if we were going out tomorrow night and will undoubtedly be pushing it.

Millie rolls her eyes at me. "We'll be back in time, Cinderella," she teases as we walk past the hotel, turn the corner, and walk right into a brick wall.

"Ooomph." I'm stumbling back from the force when I feel strong hands grip my arms. Millie lists sideways into Kenna who catches her easily.

"Whoa, Smalls. Easy." Benny steadies me, a little flash of teeth and a barely there smile drawing my attention and distracting me from the new nickname he's given me. "Where're you going in such a hurry?"

"We're not in a hurry. You're just in the way," Millie bites out.

I'm a little dazed, but I'm not sure if it's the feel of his hands on my bare skin, the smell of clean sweat coming off him, or that I seriously feel like I just took a line drive to the solar plexus. What the hell is he made of?

He ignores my sisters snipping and squats a bit so that we're at eye level. "You okay?" His hat is turned backward, the long strands of his chestnut-colored hair licking at his ears, and the brim resting on his nape. It takes me a second to gather my wits, but I shake my head and take a step back, breaking contact. "Yeah, sorry. You knocked the breath from me." My laugh is strained. I can feel all eyes on me, and it's unnerving. Almost as unnerving as realizing that he's not wearing a shirt. His shorts hang low on his hips, the band of his underwear visible, a white shirt tucked into the waistband at his back and sweat glistening on his muscular chest. A chest I'm staring at, and if the little flex he did is any indication, he knows it. Shit.

"Put some clothes on, geez!" Millie complains.

"Please don't," Lakyn says. If he hears them, he doesn't show it.

"I make you breathless, Smalls?" His smile widens, a wicked twist of lips that draws my attention away from his torso, though I'm not sure it's any safer.

"Nice try, Hayes." I pretend to play it cool when I feel anything but. "What are you doing out here, you following me?"

"Not yet."

What does that even mean?

He crosses his arms over his chest. "The gym at our hotel is being cleaned, so I went for a run."

"It's like eleventy million degrees out." That might be a bit of an exaggeration. It's more like a very warm eighty, but not by much. It's supposed to be cooler, but it's not. It's so not. Just standing here, I can feel a trickle of perspiration travel between my boobs. The heat is the reason my hair is piled on top of my head in a messy bun, there was no way I would get the wavy strands tamed here. Apparently, my hair doesn't like the dry heat any more than it likes the humidity. "And don't even say it's dry heat so it doesn't count," I admonish before he gets the chance to say exactly that.

"Oh, it counts." Benny laughs. "After being in Boston for so long, it counts. I like a good workout, though. Is it even good if you're not sweaty as fuck when you're finished?" he asks a little smugly. Is he flirting with me? Or is this just Benny Hayes being Benny Hayes?

There's a small whimper behind me, my guess it came from Kenna, followed by a snort of disgust. Millie.

"Oh, my god! Stop flirting with my sister. And seriously, go put a shirt on." My twin reaches past him and grabs my arm, pulling me away. "Let's go, Maeve."

"Bye ladies, behave yourselves," Benny calls after us as I will myself not to turn back and look. But I do it anyway. In the middle of the sidewalk in the warm Phoenix sun, hands planted on his hips, bare chest glistening in all its sweaty, muscled glory, he stands there staring at my ass. I don't know whether to be pissed off, flattered, or turned on. I think I might be all three. And also in trouble.

4

BENNY

I'd much rather be on the ice than sitting my ass outside on these bleachers in the early morning sun. At least it hasn't reached crazy high temperatures, but it's still hot. Figures that the first time I make it home in a while, we would have some record-breaking heat wave happening. This heat blows, even for Phoenix. Still, it's better than the summer when it's already hot enough to fry eggs on the sidewalk by eight in the morning. You'd think after living here my whole life I'd be used to this heat by now, but after spending so much time in the cold rinks, I don't think I ever really acclimated to the level of hell that Arizona can be. It's fucking winter, and it's supposed to be much, *much* cooler right now, which is one of the reasons they do these clinics this time of year. Clearly, we're not getting any of that weather. I promised my sister I would help her out, though, so I'm stuck here for the next couple of hours at the very least. The girls have a game first thing, and then three different clinics today, so I told Olivia I would stay for the game and then come back later. Even though it's only across the street, the chaperones and coaches are responsible for getting the players back to the hotel since it's technically off campus.

Quite a few people are in the stands as the players take the field. A lot of them are other players, both softball and baseball, but there are more people than I thought. Some even look like they may be scouts. I scan the girls, looking for Maeve as they're huddled together. The name on the back of their black jerseys is not going to be any help since I don't know what number is hers and which is Millie's. I've been to a couple of games with Levi and the rest of the guys, but I can honestly say I wasn't paying that much attention to either twin. Especially not with their brother sitting right next to me. There's a Sexton with the number ten emblazoned in white and red on her back and then right next to her is another Sexton with the number one. I'm surprised that I'm immediately certain which is which.

They break apart and start off for their positions on the diamond. "Let's go number one!" Fingers tucked into my mouth, I let out a sharp whistle. Maeve doesn't glance up, but I know she heard me when she hesitated for the briefest moment. She's not the only one who heard. Even from here, I can see the evil eye Millie is giving me. Maeve takes her place at third base, focused on the girl stepping into the batter's box. The one I should be watching. Instead, I can't take my eyes off the girl on third. She's got her legs planted wide as she focuses, waiting for whatever play comes her way. Her black hat pulled low to shade her eyes, a black and red glove at the ready. Their uniforms consist of black on black with red accent sleeves and socks, and Fulton spelled out across her chest in the same red. As an athlete myself, seeing her in her element, ready to kick ass and take names, is fucking hot. And I know that it shouldn't be. Or at least not to me, but that's where I'm at right now.

The crack of the ball against the bat drags my attention away as I follow the ball until it's caught by the left fielder for the out. After the play is made, I go back to watching Maeve, still focused, still hot, still off-limits. Maybe that's my problem. We always want what we can't have, and I for sure can't have

Levi Sexton's little sister. I pry my gaze away from her and instead force myself to watch Lakyn over on first base where it's safer. It lasts only a few seconds, though. My eyes make their way back to Maeve, and I'm reminded of the way she felt slamming into me last night. Her soft curves meeting my hard planes with absolutely no resistance. Knocking the wind right out of her gave me a reason to put my hands on her wicked soft skin. The freckles from her face traveling down her neck and spanning her chest and shoulders and down her arms. I've never seen so many freckles in all my life. It was like a constellation across her skin. A constellation I wanted to trace.

A cheer through the stands brings me out of my head to see that the Fire made quick work of the first inning and were headed off the field and into the dugout to bat. I watched as the girls took their at bats, one by one until finally, Maeve stepped up to the plate with a runner on second and two outs. My hands clasped, dangling between my legs, and I bit my lip to keep quiet. I didn't want to make her nervous by calling out to her or whistling like I wanted to. She looked dialed into the pitcher, her face set in concentration. That's one good thing about a hockey game, the glass gives you a level of separation from the spectators and makes it a little harder to hear anything over just the noise. Everyone is loud—the music, the people banging on the glass, and the cheering—but it's a lot harder to make out what any one person is saying. Here, though, you could hear a pin drop right now. The only sounds came from the other games happening on the other two fields, the birds in the trees bordering the stands, and the girls calling out encouragement to each other every so often. It's a totally different atmosphere than I'm used to.

The pitcher throws her first pitch. The slap of the ball hitting the catcher's mitt followed by a, "Striiikkke," from the ump has me sitting up straighter. "Come on, Maeve. Next one's for you," I mutter under my breath. These games don't count for anything really, so I'm not sure why I'm so anxious. The girl winds up again and releases, the yellow ball a barely visible streak through the air. Maeve lifts her left foot just a bit, and I know she's going to swing. Her bat connects, and the ball goes sailing out into left field over the head of the girl there. The Fire girls explode into cheers and yells. Maeve drops her bat and hauls ass around the bases, watching for the play to come infield so she isn't tagged out. It never comes, and she rounds home just after the girl who was on second. One by one, her teammates slap her ass as she makes her way through the dugout to my sister, who gives her a high five. Never in my life have I wanted to be a girl. Or even a softball player. The sudden jealousy over their ability to play smack ass with Maeve has me wishing I was both right now, and that's my cue to get the hell out of here for a while and find some ice. The sun is clearly getting to me.

After a detour back to the hotel where I'm staying even though my parents live less than ten minutes away, for my hockey bag and stick, I was able to score some ice time on campus between practices. The coach was one of my coaches while I was in high school; one who had hoped I would come to his team at the university once I graduated along with a lot of my teammates. My plan was always to go to Fulton, though. Their hockey program was the best, and I knew if I wanted to make it to the show eventually, that's where I needed to be. I wasn't drafted right out of high school like Levi and one of our other roommates. I had to bide my time, play some Juniors, which is where Coach Kiehn from Fulton found me and secured my decision that that was where I wanted to play. Halfway through the season my freshman year on the Fire, I was signed to a professional team. Now I just have to keep up my grades, keep up my game, and wait for them to call me up the day I graduate.

I'm just bullshitting with a couple of my old high school

teammates who stayed on the ice with me after their practice when my phone starts ringing from inside my bag. Seeing that it's my sister, I'm guessing I'm late for my chaperoning duties. "Shit, I have to take this. I'll talk to you guys later. Let me know if you wanna play while I'm in town." They agree, and we exchange fist bumps as I answer the call. "Hey, Liv. I'm on my way back now. I'm just on the other side of campus at the rink."

"I should have known." Yeah, she should have. "Just be back here in the next five minutes. They just got off the field now. Once the girls all get back to the hotel, you can go back to playing hockey or whatever." She's still disappointed I didn't take up baseball so that we had something in common. Our ten-year age gap means we didn't have a whole lot to bond over until she started coaching at FU five years ago. She was the one who encouraged me to look into the school in the first place.

"I'll be there in three!" I promise.

"Perfect. If you don't see me, just grab a group of girls and start heading back. Between the three of us, you should only have to take one group."

"Got it. I won't let anyone get lost, I swear," I tell her jokingly. This is the first year my sister has been in charge of this trip all on her own, and she's a little uptight about it.

"Make sure that you don't. And make sure you get them to the hotel but not into their rooms, Benny," Olivia warns.

"You make me sound like a predator."

"Eww, predators are creepy. You're just...you. And I've seen where that has gotten you." I'm pretty sure that was a compliment. Pretty sure.

I'm rounding the clubhouse where the teams are when I see the twins, Kenna, and Lakyn come out. "Gotta go, Liv. I found the group I want."

"Why don't I like the sound of that?"

"Probably because you're smart."

I pick up my pace, watching Maeve with her sister and

friends. She's in a pair of cut-off sweat shorts, the frayed edges hitting mid-thigh instead of at her ass cheeks like the other girls. A black cropped tank top with FU FIRE in red glitter gives me a teasing look at the pale skin of her toned stomach, and her hair is piled in a mess on top of her head. She's hotter than any girl on the team, and that includes her identical twin. I'm not sure how that works, but it's the damn truth.

Maeve turns like she senses me coming. She chews on her bottom lip as she watches me make my way toward them. I'm not sure if that's because I make her nervous, or hot, or maybe just indifferent. Whatever it is, I like it. I like that I throw her off just as much as she throws me off. If we're both off our game, nobody has an advantage.

5

MAEVE

"Maeve, will you help me with mine next?" Kenna pops her head into the bathroom where I'm putting the finishing touches on Millie's makeup. I love playing with makeup. Thankfully, they love me doing their faces as much as I enjoy doing it.

"Yeah, Ken. Give me just a sec." With a critical eye, I take in my sister's deep red lips and shimmery eye shadow before I spritz her with setting spray. I went totally opposite with my own nude lip and smoky eye. Same with our hair—she went down and wavy, and I had Lakyn do two Dutch braids. The girl is a hair wizard. Millie and I look so much alike, the matching bar necklaces, mine with my name and her with hers were our only tells most days. So I like to make whatever changes I can to make us stand out from each other. Which is why when she showed up in an outfit almost identical to mine, I changed into another one of my rompers. This one was black and white with spaghetti straps and a lacy hemline. A little shorter than I normally go, but Millie assured me that with cute strappy sandals, it was hot, not skanky, and there was absolutely no ass cheek showing. I'm not sure I believe her, though.

"Thanks, sissy," my most likely lying sister says as she poses in the mirror taking selfies of her freshly made-up face.

"You're welcome, now get out of here so I can do Kenna's, and then we can leave," I say, shooing her out as Kenna squeezes in. "What do you want me to do with you, Ken?" My eyes roam over her high cheekbones and obsidian eyes and her yellow skirt and hope she'll let me bust out my canary yellow shadow.

"Don't make me look like a ho." Easy enough. Since that was her only request, I excitedly pull out all the products I want to use. "And be quick." I nod, knowing I have to be fast because we were supposed to be gone a half hour ago.

"I'm really glad you decided to come with us to this party. I was worried after today's game you would bail. You were in beast mode!" Kenna says, her eyes closed to allow me to prime her face. "Did you see Josh and the other guys in the stands watching?" Josh is the guy whose party we're going to tonight. He seems nice. Super cute with moppy blond hair and gray eyes. He's a catcher like Kenna, but I'm pretty sure he's trying to hook up with Millie.

"I did notice them." And Benny. "I didn't get a chance to talk to them when you guys did, though. I had to go see Hannah to see if she brought any of that magic muscle cream. My hamstring was killing me."

"You could ask Benny to massage it. He looked like he was gonna eat you up right on the sidewalk yesterday!" She waggles her brows and peeps at me through a slitted eye before closing it again quickly.

"Benny is not massaging anything, and he damn sure didn't want to eat anything yesterday." Even repeating what she said has me blushing. I'm glad her eyes are closed because there's no way to hide a blush on me. My freckles practically jump off my face.

"He did too, and you would have let him if Millie wasn't

there giving you guys the stink eye." I can't even deny it. Benny had me more than just a little out of breath on that sidewalk, and it wasn't only the Arizona sun that had me hot and bothered.

"Stop talking, I need to do your face." She smirks knowingly. Kenna knows me almost as well as my sister does. I'm not fooling her by changing the subject.

FRATERNITY VILLAGE WAS a lot like our own Fraternity Row. A small area about a half mile from campus where the fraternities all had houses. We even had the Jock Jungle where a majority of our athletes who lived off campus stayed, like my brother and Benny. Their place was called Hockey House, which was totally fitting. This one is called Kegger Kastle, according to the sign out front. No red flag there or anything. "Is this really where we're going?" I question as we step from the Uber.

"Sure is," Millie singsongs as she links arms with me. She clearly isn't fazed by the name. "Okay, who is tonight's sober sitter?" Kenna asks, looking at me hopefully. Whenever we go out somewhere, we always have one person who doesn't drink and is, therefore, the sober sitter. I usually volunteer because, for one, I'm not trying to get busted for underage drinking or have someone slip me something, and for two, I'm not a beer girl, and that's usually what they have at these frat parties. When we're at my brother's, I don't have to worry about any of that. My brother doesn't really let us drink there, but when we do, I know it's the safest place to drink on campus. Neither he nor his roommates would ever let anything happen to us. As much as Millie bitches about the hockey boys, I've always appreciated having them around even if I'd never admit it to her.

There are three sets of expectant eyes on me. "Tag, I'm it." I laugh, honestly not minding.

"Yay," Kenna says, and they all give a little happy clap.

"You really are the best, Maeve," Lakyn says as she slips her arm through mine. "And you look hot as hell tonight! Who did your hair?" she teases. Talk about hot. Lakyn should be a model with her beautiful coppery skin, golden eyes, and waist-length braids. Her mother was a model in Barbados before she got married and moved to Boston. Lakyn definitely got her looks. I pale in comparison. Literally. My skin is the color of milk on a good day, and my freckles splattered across it are the only color at all.

"You're a sweet talker, Miss Alleyne." I hip bump her as the four of us pick our way across the lawn and up to the door. The music pulses from the open windows along with the sounds of laughing and talking mingled with the scent of pot and beer. Not unpleasant but it definitely sets the tone for the kind of party this is going to be.

At the door is a big, burly guy, probably a football player if I had to guess. "You ladies are new. How'd you hotties hear about this party?" His smile is wolfish as he takes us in.

"Josh told us to come by." My voice is just this side of bitchy. I'm not used to having to explain myself, and I'm not in love with the way he's checking us out.

I'm not sure if it's my tone or if it's the mention of Josh's name, but he stops ogling long enough to wave us in. "He's in there somewhere."

Without bothering to thank him, I move aside so the girls can go ahead of me and follow behind them. Knowing he's watching has me wishing for my brother and his hockey boys. Maybe I should have invited Benny. It's not the first time I thought about it. I almost asked him yesterday when he walked us back to the hotel. He had been covered in sweat again with a white tee clinging to his muscled arms and chest, his hockey bag slung over a shoulder, and his hat twisted backward. A rapid heartbeat and what felt like a flock of birds in my belly had me off balance. So much so that I started telling him about our plans. My sister was not affected by the sight of Benny Hayes, though, and she shut me up real quick with a vicious jab of her elbow in my ribs. Now I'm wishing I had fought through the sting and told him. Since Millie told me about this party, I had been worried about the sorority sisters not welcoming us, but I never gave any thought to the guys being *too* welcoming. Just another reminder of the safety net my brother has created for us on the FU campus.

Leaning into Millie so I can be heard, I say, "Hey, try not to drink here tonight. I don't trust these guys."

"Oh, sissy, you worry too damn much." She tugs at my hand, dragging me toward the doorway that presumably leads to the kitchen and typically the drinks. As we make our way through, my unease at not knowing anyone here at all grows. There are some appreciative and curious looks from the guys at the party, and some not so appreciative looks from the ladies. This is going to be a long night.

About two hours later, I'm making my way through the house, a little more familiar with the layout, to find Lakyn and my sister. Kenna hasn't left my side all that much. She's not feeling the crowd here any more than I am. We've danced a little and chatted with some other softball players we recognized from the field, but we've mostly spent our time wandering around the house and the backyard where a pool and hot tub full of nearly naked bodies is located. There are just as many people in the pool as there are in the house, and that is saying a lot. It's surprising since the cool desert air is enough to cause goose bumps to blossom across my skin the minute I stepped foot onto the terra-cotta pool deck. I had to be careful not to slip on the wet tiles. Who tiles by a pool anyway? I pick my way through the people milling about, looking for

Lakyn's long braids or my sister's red waves. It shouldn't be this hard to find them, and that has me a little concerned.

"Do you think they left?" Kenna, shouts over the thumping bass.

"No, they wouldn't do that." I'm certain of it. My sister might be a little on the wild side at times, but she's not stupid, and neither is Lakyn.

The pad of my thumb caught between my teeth as I nibble away at the softball-roughened skin and continue to scan the crowd.

"There!" I point over at a massive potted cactus to where Lakyn and Millie are standing, red Solo cups in hand talking to three guys. Two I recognize from the fields, Josh and Marcus, but the third I don't know. Just by my sister's body movements, I can tell that she's at least a little tipsy, if not bordering on drunk. With a sigh, I grab Kenna's hand and start picking our way around everyone, praying the whole way I don't somehow end up in the pool.

"Hey, sissy!" Millie slurs slightly, her skin flushed and eyes a bit glassy.

"Holy shit," the one I don't know says. "There are two of you?"

Josh just laughs. "I told you, Shane! I thought I was seeing things at first."

"Wow," the guy, Shane, says again, taking us both in from head to toe. Slowly.

"You okay?" I ask both my sister and Lakyn, ignoring his eyes on me.

"We're good, Maevey. Promise," Lakyn says, clearly *way* more sober than my sister but still buzzed.

Marcus stands with his hand on her hip, saying something in Lakyn's ear and not paying much attention to the rest of us standing there. She laughs at whatever he's saying and starts to walk off with him, snagging Kenna's wrist and dragging her with. At least I knew Kenna had Lakyn, so I could focus on Millie.

"Yeah, Maevey," Shane mimics. "They're good. They're big girls."

My sister giggles at that, leaning back into Josh, who steadies her by pulling her into his chest.

"Cool it, Shane. She's just looking out for them," Josh tells his asshole friend, giving me an apologetic look.

"You don't trust us?" he asks, stepping closer. "Afraid we might bite?" He snaps his teeth at me and laughs.

"I don't know you, so no, I don't trust you, but I'm definitely not afraid of you either," I tell him with as much Boston as I can inflect in my voice. Hopefully, it makes me sound tougher than I am. I don't like this guy.

He raises his hands, palms out. "Whoa, don't kick my ass, girl!" Shane says innocently. "Come on, Millie." I turn my shoulder on him and extend my hand to her.

"Awwww, Maeve. Just a little while longer?" she pleads.

"Let me get you a drink. Just hang out for a little bit." Josh tries to soften the douchiness of his friend with a peace offering and a smile.

"Oooh, I want a drink!" my sister says excitedly.

I roll my eyes because I'm not getting out of here anytime soon. She definitely doesn't need any more to drink, but there's no way I'll convince her of that just yet. "I'll get the drinks. Where will you be?" The question is directed at Josh. At this point, between him and Mill, I'm only going to get straight answers from him, and I'm not asking Shane shit. I don't want to encourage or engage. Josh glances around and points at an empty pub table in the corner of the patio.

I nod. "I'll be right back. Watch my sister, Josh." He smiles reassuringly, leading her to the table. His asshole friend follows. Unfortunately. If he thinks I'm going to warm up toward him and we're going to hook up or something, he's dead ass wrong.

Not wanting to let my sister out of my sight for too long, I start weaving quickly through the crowd to the kitchen, resigned to the fact that I'm going to be here for a while yet. Millie is going to owe me big time.

6

BENNY

With my windows rolled down, I navigate the back streets, enjoying the quiet and the sweet smell of creosote in the air. A lot different from the sounds and smells of the city. Luckily, my dad thought to drop my old car off at the hotel for me earlier so that I could use it while I'm here. I got a new whip my sophomore year at FU, something better for the Boston winters. He kept this one for a backup and to take the dogs for a ride, he said, so that he wouldn't have to put them in his Audi. That explains the lint brush, the shedding beasts, and the slight smell of the special dog shampoo my mom uses on them.

I could have walked the short distance from the hotel to this party, but I knew I wouldn't be drinking tonight, and I didn't want to get eaten by a damn coyote or some shit on my way home later, so I drove. Trying to find parking is a bitch, though. I'm just circling back around when I get lucky, and somebody pulls out right in front. I'm actually surprised at the number of people here because most students don't stick around for the breaks. I pocket my keys and take the porch steps two at a time.

They usually have one of the new pledges or one of the football players at the door for crowd control at these parties, but there's nobody, so I walk right in.

"Benny fucking Hayes! I heard you were in town!" I turn when I hear my name and groan inwardly. Of all people.

"'Sup, man." I lift my chin by way of greeting.

"Bro! I'm glad you came; it's been a minute since you've been home. You picked a good party too," Matt goes on animatedly. "Josh invited a bunch of softball chicks, and I heard there are some fucking hot ginger twins. I'm about to find them and show them how welcoming we can be at Kegger Kastle." He rubs his hands together, not realizing he just fucked up. "Who you here with? You come alone?"

The girls are here? I scan the room looking for them before I settle back on him, my expression blank. "Nah, I'm not alone."

Matt looks around behind me expectantly. "You come with Blayne and them?" He mentions my old teammates, the ones I had played with yesterday. They actually told me about this party. They're the obvious choice since we rarely went anywhere without each other when I lived here.

"Nope. I came with the fucking hot ginger twins," I answer flatly, throwing his words back at him. I never did like this motherfucker.

"The twins? Both of them?" He looks a little nervous now.

"Both of them. Best tell your boys." I didn't have beef with any of the Delta guys but knowing that Maeve is here and that she and Millie are being talked about among the brothers... well, it's never too late to make enemies, I guess.

"No problem, Benny. You always were lucky like that," Matt says wryly, trying to lighten the mood. It's too late, though. He's already set the mood for the night, and it's not good. "They're here somewhere with a couple of friends. Probably with Josh since he invited them."

Josh, I know and liked, so that was a plus. He's a good guy

and wouldn't get the twins into any trouble. "I'll find them." With a tip of my chin as way of a goodbye and thanks, I head off to look for Maeve. It shouldn't be that hard to find her. Not too many identical twins with flaming red hair hanging around. After walking the whole first floor and second and not finding the girls, I head out to the pool area. I've been stopped at least a dozen times by people welcoming me home, offering me drinks, and some even trying to drag me upstairs to one of the rooms for a quick blow job. Gotta love sheltered daddy's girls turned college girls. They're the wildest. On my way out to the patio, I notice the steam misting off the pool, the heaters working hard in the chilly desert night. Ducking my head as I walk through the sliding doors, my eyes go straight to all the bodies playing in the water, and I hope to fuck Maeve isn't one of them. I've never thrown someone over my shoulder all caveman like, but I think seeing her in a bathing suit frolicking around with some fucking frat boy would push me right over the edge. Thankfully, I don't see her or her sister in the pool. I scan the rest of the patio and finally spot Lakyn and Kenna walking back into the house but not the twins. I'm starting to get a little worried now. The only thing that has me relatively calm is that I checked the bedrooms upstairs and didn't find them there either. I saw a few bare asses and more than one chick on her knees, but none of them were Maeve, and that was all I cared about. I'm not even going to try to explain that to myself. Just as I'm about to go ask Kenna if they know where Maeve is, there's a loud squeal over in the corner that draws my attention. Across the pool, I see braided red hair and lacy black shorts that barely cover her ass. An ass that is being covertly appreciated by some douche standing with her, Josh, and a drunk-looking Millie. My temper has been on simmer since I walked in the front door, but from the rigid set of her shoulders, she's clearly uncomfortable, so it's about two seconds away from boiling over. Not stopping until I'm standing right behind them, I slip my hand to Maeve's nape. Cupping the creamy freckled covered skin gently and possessively as I lock eyes with the dick who was just checking her ass out. Maeve startles but only slightly before she settles into my touch. My glare is full of challenge and a whole lot of "I wish you would." When his eyes dart away from mine, I snort out a curt laugh. Pussy.

"Hey, Smalls," I say quietly, glancing down at her with a reassuring smile. She turns into me a bit, and the smile she gives me is tight, but the relief of my being there is evident on her face. I can feel the guy's eyes on us again, probably trying to figure out what's going on, and if he's going to have to find another hookup for the night. He absolutely fucking is. Without thought and as if I have every right to, I bend and gently, so as not to mess up her pretty lipstick, place my lips over Maeve's. Just that slight touch of our mouths has me feeling as if I was slammed into the boards by a two-hundred-and-fifty-pound goon out on the ice. Only I like this a whole lot more. Not ready to stop kissing her but not sure how she's going to react, I reluctantly begin to straighten, nipping at her full bottom lip as I do. Before I can pull away, Maeve tangles her fingers into my hair and brings me back down. My eyes widen in surprise, but when she looks up at me through the curtain of her thick lashes, I see the same want there that's coursing through my veins right now, so I open for her, letting her take what she wants. When our lips meet again, Maeve's mouth parts on a gasp. I smile, pressing her tighter against my chest and dip my tongue to brush against hers. Only enough to tease us both. Once, twice, three times. Slowly, she pulls back, and I straighten. Smirking at the dazed look on Maeve's face, I hope that I'm not sporting the same expression because I sure as fuck feel dazed.

Like we didn't just kiss each other both stupid, I turn to give

Josh knuckles and find Millie with her mouth hanging open in shock.

"What's up, Josh?" We bump fists inches from Millie's surprised face.

"Heard you were on this trip with the softball team. Your sister's one of the coaches, right?" he asks, settling his hand back on Millie's waist. She still looks a little stunned but not uncomfortable or anything, so I decide to leave it alone. His friend with the staring problem was a different story, though.

With an arm hooked around Maeve's waist, I settle her in front of me, her back to my chest. I widen my legs to make room for her between them and cross my arms across her middle, leaving absolutely no question that she's with me. When she doesn't stiffen and instead molds into me, I answer him. "Yeah. I lucked out and got to chaperone." I glance over at Josh's friend, still standing there watching us. If I were him, I would have bailed the minute I walked up. Clearly, he's not real smart. "Do I know you, bro?" I ask him.

"Oh, my bad. Shane, this is one of my friends, Benny Hayes. We go way back. He played hockey at the high school when Coach was there," Josh says to me. "Shane plays here for Coach Metzger."

Shane smiles a little like he's just been handed a piece of candy or something. "That's cute. You played high school hockey."

Josh tries to interrupt, "N-" I put my hand up to stop him, hoping this asshole is going to put his foot in his mouth.

"Couldn't get on the team here?" he says smugly.

There it is. I was waiting for this shit. The chance to make him look stupid, and he's doing it all on his own. Payback for thinking he was gonna hook up with Maeve and for checking out her ass behind her fucking back.

"Didn't try. I got picked up out of Juniors by Fulton University." The smugness slips from his face at the mention of Junior hockey and then FU. Their hockey team is top-notch, and anyone who knows hockey knows it. "Got drafted to Boston my sophomore year. I'm going to the show right after graduation, so I guess you could say I'm too good for the team here." His face is a mask of embarrassment and hatred. I'm not sure which is stronger. He goes to leave, not even bothering to respond, but I call him back. "Yo! Shane."

"What?"

"Keep your fucking eyes to yourself next time." My jaw is pulsing as I stare him down. I'm madder than I should be about the whole thing. I've done the same thing to chicks more times than I can count. Hell, I've done it to Maeve.

Maeve wriggles in my arms, she has to feel the tension in my body facing off with him right now. For the first time since I've walked up, she speaks. "Benny, will you help me find Kenna and Lakyn? We have to leave soon. We're already way past curfew." I break eye contact with Shane, giving him the out to walk away, and look down at her upturned face. Her neck craned to connect with me.

"I don't wanna leave, sissy." Millie pouts, but Maeve shoots her down.

"No choice, Mill."

"I can bring her home later." At Josh's offer, Millie peps up, and again, Maeve shoots her down.

"Nope. If I go, we go. You know the rules."

Like someone kicked her puppy, Millie steps out of Josh's arms and pecks his cheek. "I'll text you later." He nods and releases his hold on her. She takes one step and stumbles. Maeve and I both reach for her, and immediately, I miss the heat of her body tucked into mine.

"Come on, drunky poo." Maeve laughs, hooking her arm with Millie's.

With another fist bump to Josh, I lead the girls away, my hand on the small of Maeve's back. She lets me steer them toward the house. Millie's bitching the whole time about what party poopers we are. "Hey! What are you doing kissing my sister?" she demands, stopping dead in her tracks and almost causing me to run them both over.

Maeve doesn't look at me, just stares straight ahead. "Because I wanted to," I answer honestly. "And that fuck head, Shane, was eye fucking her when I walked up."

"He was not!" Millie insists. Maeve stiffens. She knows he was. I could see the unease in her from across the fucking yard.

"He was. Not that I'm surprised." I roll my eyes and lean closer to be heard over the loud music, putting me in contact with Maeve again. "You know every guy's fantasy is sleeping with twins, right? I mean you have to know that. And then you two show up here looking like this?" I wave a hand to encompass the two of them and their little outfits and done up hair and makeup. Maeve looks like a wet fucking dream, my wet fucking dream. Millie looks hot, but I'm having a hard time seeing her as anything other than Levi's little sister. I'm not having that problem with Maeve anymore, though. And that's a problem within itself. "Yeah, your brother was right to tell me to watch you." Fucking A right he was.

"Ewww, you guys are gross," Millie says, a disgusted look wrinkling her face.

"Gross or not, it's the truth," I assure her. And it is. Tapping twins was one of mine until about ten minutes ago when I realized the only Sexton twin I wanted to get naked with was Maeve.

"That's enough, you two; let's get Kenna and Lakyn and get back to the hotel."

"How'd you guys get here?" I ask, hoping she's not going to say that they walked.

"Uber," Maeve says, standing on her tiptoes to get a better view of the party. "There they are." She points.

"Let's go." I tuck her tiny hand into mine, clasping my

fingers around hers and pull her in the direction of the exit, stopping only to snag Kenna and Lakyn from the two guys they were in the corner making out with. I don't think I've ever been the responsible one in all my damn life, but here I am, herding four girls out of a frat party and not to smash.

7

MAEVE

"So are we going to talk about what happened last night?" Millie asks from across the bench in the locker room. I was wondering how long it would take her to bring it up. Longer than I thought actually.

"Nothing happened," I lie. Whatever happened wasn't nothing. Not to me.

"What did we miss?" Kenna asks, coming over with Lakyn right behind. They plop down on the bench next to where I sit tying my cleats.

"Nothing," I repeat. "Millie was drunk and is imagining shit." My sister is never going to let this go.

"Like hell, I imagined it. Benny Hayes kissed my sister at Josh's party last night, and she's trying to play it off like it's no big deal."

"Because it isn't," I interject.

"Wait, wait, wait. You kissed your brother's roommate?" Lakyn asks before hooting in laughter. "Oh my god, you guys are so dead." She continues laughing.

Standing, I put my stuff in the locker and shut it with a clang. "Nobody is getting dead; it was no big deal. He only kissed me because some asshole was hitting on me, and I couldn't just walk away because Millie wasn't ready to leave. Plus, she was drunk as hell, so I couldn't leave her alone. That's it." That may be why *he* kissed me, but Shane had nothing to do with the reason I kissed him. Done talking about this, I try to make my escape. We have a game starting in a few minutes, which will give me a little bit of a reprieve from the grilling in here.

"Girlfriend! You were kissing on one of the hockey boys! One of the hottest guys on campus! It's totally a big deal," Lakyn says, grinning from ear to ear. "Maeve Sexton being a bad girl. It's about damn time."

I just roll my eyes. "You guys are making a big deal out of nothing." I feel like a broken record. Maybe if I say it enough, I'll start to believe it too.

"I knew it. I knew you liked him." Kenna claps gleefully.

"Why are you guys encouraging her?" Millie demands, her hands planted on her hips, her scowl fierce.

"Because he's fine as hell, and Maeve clearly likes him," Kenna says, joining me at the door. "She wouldn't have let him kiss her if she didn't." She slaps my butt and pushes the door open, letting in the bright sunlight and temporarily blinding me.

"I do not like him. It was just a—a diversion." I'm grasping with that one.

"Whatever you say, Maeve." Lakyn winks, following us out the door with my sulking sister bringing up the rear.

We walk around the corner to head out to the field and nearly plow into Benny. He has a really bad habit of being in the way. "Oh shit," I mutter under my breath. Was he standing here the whole time? Could he hear us talking? What is he doing here? He's been playing hockey every morning and meeting us after the clinics to walk us back to the hotel. It's the only reason I was even able to focus. That first day when he sat in the stands cheering for me, my nerves were so frayed I could barely concentrate.

"Morning, ladies." He greets us all, but his eyes are on me. I avert my gaze before I do something silly like kiss him again. How does he look so good in the most basic clothes? A plain white tee, Under Armour shorts, and his ever-present backward FU hat never looked so good on anybody in the history of ever.

"Stalker much?" Millie bites out.

"You wish, Off-limits," Benny tells her. I cringe at the nickname. A blatant reminder.

"You weren't calling us that last night when you were kissing my sister."

Benny shrugs. "She's Smalls. You're Off-limits," he answers smoothly as if that explains everything. It explains nothing.

Before I even have a chance to try to dissect the meaning behind that or say anything to him, a blur in the form of a girl comes flying through the air out of nowhere and literally tackles Benny. Thankfully, he's solid and is able to stay upright. She gives a little squeal as she wraps her legs around his waist, her arms around his neck, and her mouth lands right. On. His.

I blink rapidly, trying to figure out if I'm really watching him kiss another girl right in front of me. My face is awash with confusion and hurt that I do my best to mask. Who is this?

Benny turns his face, breaking their kiss, and starts to untangle her limbs from his.

"Friend of yours?" Millie asks with disdain, her arms crossed over her chest, her brows disappearing under the brim of her hat.

Doing my best not to let him see my reaction, I straighten my spine, standing as tall as I can, and bite the inside of my cheek to keep me from saying something I'll regret later. I feel like such an idiot.

When he finally gets her back on her feet, he moves her to

his side. Wiping a hand over his mouth does nothing but smear the bubblegum pink lipstick she left behind.

"Samantha, what are you doing here?" He doesn't sound thrilled to see her, but that could just be wishful thinking on my part. Or maybe he's pissed that he just got busted in front of the girl he was kissing only a few hours ago.

She links her arm through his and gazes up at him adoringly while the four of us stand here unable to look away from them. "Josh told me that you were here chaperoning for Liv, so I decided to come down and see you." Smoothing a hand over his chest, she pouts. "Why didn't you text me and tell me you were in town? I would have come right over."

I've seen enough and officially feel like the side chick although that's just stupid since all it was, was a little kiss. Lakyn and Kenna are flanking me with my sister standing to the side of us. "I'll meet you out on the field, guys."

"Smalls!" Benny takes a step toward me, but Samantha doesn't let go of his arm.

"The game's going to start without them if they don't hurry, Ben," she tells him. "We can go watch or make out under the bleachers like we used to in high school," she practically purrs. I'm no dummy. Samantha is doing it for our benefit. Staking her claim. Well, she can have him.

"She's right, *Ben*," I say with a saccharine sweet smile. "We have to go. Come on, girls. Looks like they have some catching up to do." I'm so proud of myself for keeping the wobble out of my voice when it was so close to the surface. I cannot believe I let him play me. It might have only been a kiss, but it was one kiss too damn many.

With my head held high and my girls by my side, I walk past them and out onto the field. I need to focus on the ball. I should have never let Benny Hayes get in my head. I know better. Boys and ball don't mix. Especially when that boy is Benny Hayes.

Bottom of the fifth inning, I'm more aware than I want to be of Benny and his little girlfriend in the stands. I wish they would just disappear, but instead, Benny's been there cheering since we took the field. I've not allowed myself to even glance up in his direction. The only reason I know that they're still there other than the fact that he's turned into my personal cheerleader is that either my sister, Lakyn, or Kenna have had something to say about them being there.

"Can you believe he's sitting up there with her like he wasn't kissing my fucking sister yesterday? Just wait until I tell Levi. He'll really beat his ass now!"

"Here I thought he was one of the good guys," Kenna says disappointed.

"Don't even sweat it, baby girl. He's not worth your time," Lakyn reassures.

I don't respond to any of them. Just do my best to keep my head in the game. Right now, the other team has one out and a runner on second. Eyes on the batter, I'm ready for the line drive that comes right at me after a bounce just this side of the foul line. What I'm not ready for is the player running at me, trying to tag up before I do. She plows into me with her arms extended in front of her, sending me flying and knocking every bit of air from my body. It leaves me in a great whoosh. My head thumps off the hard clay ground, and my hat falls off in the process. All I can do is lay there and try to catch my breath, the tears rolling from the corner of my eyes to mingle with the dirt and my loose hair. My eyes slowly open at the sound of my name as I struggle still to pull air into my lungs. It hurts so bad. Coach Hayes and Hannah are standing over me, concern evident on their faces. I can faintly hear Millie. She sounds a mile away, coloring the air with a string of curse words that my brother would be proud of. I'm not sure who she's talking to, but I'm guessing it's the girl who mowed me down. Mingled with the faces of my coach and trainer are little white dots that I can't seem to blink away. And a worried looking Benny.

"Maeve, can you hear me? Don't try to talk just squeeze my hand if you can," Hannah tells me. I can just barely make out what she's saying over the blood rushing through my ears, making that canned *wah, wah, wah* sound. I squeeze her hand, and she nods. "That's good. Does anything feel broken? Squeeze once for no," she instructs. Even as I squeeze no, she goes about checking my limbs one by one, followed by my collarbone, and then my head for any bleeding.

"That's good. As soon as you can catch your breath, we'll help you off the field, and I'll do a better check. Make sure you don't have a concussion or anything, okay? You just take your time; they can all wait." Hannah smiles down at me and tells Coach that I won't be back in the game today, and that the girl who ran me down should be thrown. They go on talking about it as I lie there and try to get my breathing under control, which is harder to do with Benny hovering, watching but not saying anything. After a few moments, I move to sit up, but Hannah guides me back down. "Whoa, whoa, we're gonna take it nice and easy. You took one hell of a hit, and although you may not have broken anything, you may have other injuries. We'll get you up gently." I nod my agreement but only slightly so I don't jar my head and the already blossoming headache. I'm ready for them to help me up when Benny pushes them both out of the way and gently scoops me into his arms, cradling me to him and leaving me no choice but to put my arm around his shoulder and let him take me to the locker room amid the clapping of my teammates. He's lucky I'm in too much pain to resist him right now because after earlier, I totally would. I would fight the shit out of him.

8

BENNY

Watching Maeve go down on the field today was rough. I've seen plenty of players get hurt in hockey before, but we're guys playing a contact sport, so it's expected. After that whole shit show with Samantha, I'm surprised she even let me help her off the field. But I couldn't *not* help her. I had to. The urge to sweep her up and run her to the nearest hospital was real. I managed to wait but just barely.

Hannah kicked me out of the exam room as soon as I set Maeve down on the table, and I haven't seen her since. My sister took her back to the hotel earlier. She wanted to make sure she was okay, so I took her group of girls back to the hotel before heading to my parents' for dinner, wishing I hadn't already agreed to go. Impatiently, I stab at the elevator button, not really wanting to take the stairs to the tenth floor like I do in the morning, but I will if it means I can check on Maeve faster. Just as I'm about to bail for the stairs, the elevator doors whoosh open, and I step in. They're just closing when Lakyn yells, "Hold the door." Quickly, I stick my hand out to stop the door from sliding closed. She and Kenna make a mad dash and practically tumble into the elevator laughing. They silence abruptly, and both go from smiling to glaring Millie style. "Ugh. I would have waited for the next one had I known you were in here," Lakyn says, flipping her hair over her shoulder with her hands planted on her hips.

What the fuck did I do? "Ummm...what?"

"Oh, don't act like you don't know what I'm talking about. Where's your girl now?" Her lips are pursed as she waits for my answer. Kenna's staring me down like she might actually hit me if she doesn't like my answer.

"Who are you talking about, Lakyn?" Then it dawns on me. Samantha. They're pissed because of this morning when she just showed up at the fields to stir shit. "Ahhh, Samantha. She's not my girl. Hasn't been in a long ass time."

"Sure looked like she was." Kenna's tone is hostile as fuck.

"Well, she's not. We dated in high school and broke up when I left for Boston. That's it. We hook up sometimes when I come home." When Kenna's eyes narrow into slits, I feel the need to add to that statement. "Not this time, though, and I don't have any plans to either, so you can chill." I don't know why I'm defending myself to them. I don't owe them any explanation, but clearly, they're pissed. My guess is it's because they heard about the kiss between Maeve and me last night, and then this morning, Sam shows up acting like she's my girlfriend. If these two are this pissed, I don't even want to know how mad the twins are. I only care about how upset one Sexton is, though.

As soon as the doors open, I head right for Maeve's room with the girls right behind me. At her room, I come to a dead stop at the sight of a red scarf hanging off her doorknob. What the fuck? At Hockey House, if one of us hangs something on our door, it means we're in there fucking. Instant anger mixed with a whole lot of jealousy bubbles up quickly. I raise my fist to pound on the door when Lakyn and Kenna both grab me and pull me away.

"That's Millie's signal, not Maeve's, you goon. Calm down."

I don't have time to be impressed by Lakyn's use of hockey terminology because my blood is pumping through my veins quicker than I want it to be. The thought that it was Maeve in there with somebody has me shook. Shocked and more than a little pissed, I ask, "She kicked her sister out after she was hurt today?"

"Maeve would just come by us," Kenna assures.

"Yeah, except you two weren't here," I point out. They both have the decency to look sheepish. "Not real fucking helpful."

"Benny, our whole team is here. It's not like we're the only people she can crash with." Kenna doesn't sound confident in that statement, which makes me feel even less than confident that she's crashing in one of her teammate's rooms.

"We'll find her. Don't worry your pretty little head over *our* girl. We *got* her." Lakyn is obviously still pissed about Samantha and not buying my story. Tough shit.

"You check with your teammates, and I'll check with my sister."

Kenna pulls her phone out. "I'll just call her." We all stand there and wait. "Voicemail."

I hold my hand out. "Gimme your phone." She hands it over reluctantly. I punch in my number and hit send. "There, now you have my number, and I have yours. If you find her first, text me."

"You'll text us then if you find her?" Nodding, I take off for the elevator, pulling my own phone out to text Liv. I don't want to get Maeve in trouble for not being in her room past curfew, and I don't want to stress my sister out either. I know her nerves were a little frayed after the accident today.

> Benny: Hey Liv! How is Maeve? Have you seen her since you guys got back?

I watch as the three dots that tell me she's typing dance across my phone.

> Olivia: She's okay. Last time I saw her, Hannah had her in the pool and hot tub to try to loosen up her muscles and keep her from being too sore tomorrow.

> Benny: Sweet. I'll see you in the morning.

> Olivia: Sleep tight, little bro. And alone! Xoxo

Skipping the elevator for the stairs, I take them two at a time to the rooftop pool. It's supposed to be closed right now, but it's worth a try. The pool and hot tub can't be seen from the door, so I step out and walk through all the patio furniture and potted palms to the other side of the L-shaped roof. Just like the other night at the party, the pool is throwing off steam in the cool air, making it look like a hot spring. Through the mist, I see a form sitting on the pool ledge, submerged to her neck. Careful not to startle her, I quietly walk closer. Maeve's eyes are closed, her pale skin glowing from the mixture of pool lights and the full moon, her red hair floating on the water around her shoulders. She looks like a mermaid. I can't tell if she's sleeping, but she still hasn't heard me approach. I squat down next to her, appreciating the tiny black crocheted bikini she's wearing. The ties at her waist floating against her thighs, drawing my attention. The triangles barely cover her tits, and I'm trying to figure out if it's her skin I can see through the material or if it's some kind of lining.

"Are you finished?" Maeve asks in a low voice, scaring the shit out of me.

"You scared me!" I chuckle. "Finished what?"

"Ogling me while I sleep." Her eyes are still closed.

"Should you sleep in a pool?" I don't bother denying that I was checking her out. She cracks an eye for a moment before closing it again. "I was doing just fine until you showed up." My phone pings in my pocket. "Your girlfriend?" Maeve asks sardonically.

"She's not my girlfriend, Smalls." The text is from Kenna wanting to know if I found her. I debate answering but don't want them to come up here.

> Benny: Yeah. All good

> Kenna: Where r u guys?

> Benny: With my sister

The lie comes easily. They won't go looking for her because they know they'll get in trouble for curfew.

"It's Kenna. They were looking for you."

"Yeah, my sister has company."

"Saw that. How do you feel?" I don't want to tell her for a split second I thought of knocking the door down when I thought it was her in there with some guy.

"Okay. Just a little sore. The water helps a lot, though. My head was what Hannah was most worried about, but I don't even have a headache."

"How's the water?" I trail my fingers through it, flicking her with the droplets clinging to the tips and smiling at her scrunched face when they hit my target.

"It's nice. Relaxing." She sits up, the water lapping at the tops of her breasts, legs kicking making gentle waves. Dying to feel their silky smoothness against me, I stand and kick of my shoes, my shirt following. I'm just pulling down my shorts when she squeaks in a panicked voice, "What are you doing, Benny?"

My hands still on my waistband. "You said the water was nice. So I'm coming in."

"With me? You can't come in here with me." Her eyes are wide and a little wild.

"Why not? You afraid I'm gonna go all baby shark and eat you?" I smirk at the flash I see in her eyes. Maeve Sexton might not like me very much at the moment, but she still wants me, and that's enough to work with. Dropping my shorts on the pile with the rest of my things, I decide to save her modest little soul by keeping on my boxers. They're white, though, and they're not going to cover much once they get wet. It won't bother me in the least, though. I've been stripping down in a locker room full of guys for over a decade now. I have zero modesty left. Toes on the edge of the deck, I dive in, swimming underwater to the end of the pool before coming up for air.

"You can just stay on that side of the pool!" she calls to me.

With a laugh and a shake of my head, I dip back under the warm water and glide over to where she's sitting. Breaking the surface right in front of where she sits on the built-in ledge. Water dripping down my face, I smooth my hair back from my eyes, dragging the water with the wet strands. I step into the space between her knees and brace my hands on the concrete deck on either side of her. "Why would I stay over there when you're all the way over here, Smalls?" She's doing her best not to touch me, and I'm doing my best to make sure she does.

"I don't know, *Ben*. Why would you want to be here with me?" She mocks me with the name that Samantha used yesterday. Literally the only person in my life who ever calls me Ben instead of Benny. Probably the reason I dislike it so much.

"You know why." I tower over Maeve normally, but with her sitting in the pool, we are closer in height but still too much to let me see into her face. Dropping down to my knees in the shallow water, I drop my arms beside her waist now, resting on the seat she's perched on. My fingers find the strings that hold her bikini bottom on and twirl them around and around. I can see the flush making its way across the creamy skin of her chest and her neck, the freckles becoming more prominent as her color rises.

"Why'd you kiss me?" Maeve's voice is hoarse. Her eyes locked on my mouth.

Tilting her chin, I force her to look me in the eye. "Because I wanted to. I've wanted to since five seconds after you sat next to me on the plane. I want to now," I finish gruffly and watch as her eyes change. The blue bursts appear lighter as her pupils darken and expand. The more I watch her, the more the colors transform. "Why did you kiss me?" I ask to remind her that she did, in fact, kiss me too.

Maeve shakes her head. "I'm not sure." The lie slips from her lips effortlessly.

"That's not true, and you know it." She averts her gaze as I call her out. Her lashes create shadows on her cheeks, water clinging to them and shimmering like diamonds in the moonlight.

She takes a deep breath as if she's summoning courage and looks back at me. "I kissed you because I wanted to, too. You made me feel safe."

"You kissed me because I made you feel safe?" I'm not sure that's a normal reaction. I needed her to have kissed me because she couldn't fucking help it. Because the desire to feel my mouth on hers was as strong as mine was. Safe?

"No. Yes. No," Maeve says, clearly flustered. "I mean, yes, you made me feel safe, and I liked feeling that way, but I also felt protected in a way that I never have. Like I belonged to you, and that made me...want to kiss you, I guess," she says a little shyly. "I mean, I know I don't, and that we're not together, but at that moment..." Her eyes dart around my face, away, back, and away again. Her timidness when talking about a kiss is fucking sexy, and it makes me wonder what talking dirty to her would be like. I should put her out of her misery, though. She's clearly not used to such direct questions.

"What about now?" I ask, tugging her a bit closer so that she can feel my hardness pressed into her, the only barrier the thin material of her bikini and the even thinner cotton of my boxers. "Do you feel like you're mine now?" My eyes drift down to watch her mouth, her tongue darting out to wet her full bottom lip. My fingers flex into the soft flesh of her hips, my restraint is barely hanging by a thread.

"I can't be." Her answer is barely audible. "My brother—"

"Isn't here. And what he doesn't know can't hurt us."

9

MAEVE

"**W**hat he doesn't know can't hurt us."

He's so right, and I'm so tempted. There's no way this could ever go any farther than here, though. I refuse to sneak around back home, and Levi would never in a million years go for me dating one of the hockey boys. My body feels overheated, and it has nothing to do with the warm water of the heated pool and everything to do with Benny Hayes and his erection pressed against me. It's literally taking everything in my power not to rub against him. Is it still considered dry humping if we're in water? The dirty thought sparks even more heat. I'm no prude, but Benny seems to bring out a side of me I'm not sure I knew I had. He makes me feel bolder than I ever have before. Sexier and in control at the same time as he makes me feel completely out of control. It's a heady mix, one I tried to ignore. Until he kissed me. Ever since that moment, it's been all I've thought about. Even when Samantha showed up, and I was hurt and embarrassed. The thought of not being able to kiss him again weighed just as heavily on my mind as the fact that he wasn't mine to kiss. Now here he is, telling me with his eyes, with his body, with his words meant to reassure, that he could be mine to kiss.

"What he doesn't know..." I trail off, lifting my face in silent invitation, hoping he understands what I'm asking for.

Benny pulls his lip between his teeth and shakes his head. "You gotta ask me for it, Smalls." His hands are at my waist toying with the ties holding my bottoms on, drawing my attention to their fiddling.

I squirm against him, causing him to hiss out and me to swallow a moan. Just that little movement shot sparks right through my core, pebbling my nipples. Once I'm able to find my voice, I demand, "Kiss me, Benny." Not even sounding like myself, I clear my throat and gather some courage to say it again. "Kiss me, please. I need you too."

Never have I been this direct, but never have I been this desperate for someone's lips on mine. He stands, the water cascading down his chest and arms, causing me to look up at him now but only for a moment. With his hands wrapped around my waist, he lifts me effortlessly off the ledge I was perched on and sits with me still in his arms. Taking my legs in his hands, he wraps them around him, positioning me onto his lap more comfortably. I can't help but look down to where the head of his erection in his now sheer white boxers rubs against the black triangle covering my center. He drapes my arms over his shoulders, letting his hands skate up my arms and across my throat to tangle in the wet ropes of my hair, tugging me tighter against him. His eyes travel over my face, the heat in them calling to me. We're so close that I can feel the rise and fall of his chest against my own. "I don't know about you, Smalls, but this feels right. This feels like you're mine," he whispers against my lips, his minty breath fanning over my mouth right before he closes the distance between us. I'm immediately pliant under his touch. My tongue darts to meet his in a duel. Lips, teeth, tongues. I slant my mouth to give him better access. I feel as if I can't get close enough. Benny's hands are kneading the globes of my ass, pressing me down harder onto his lap, rocking into me. Stars explode behind my eyelids at the delicious pressure. We break apart just long enough to drag in air, our lips crashing together once we do. His hands glide up my spine, and with quick work, he has my bikini top untied. I lean back and watch as it slips from my neck and lands between us, floating on the water. Benny grabs it up and tosses it over his shoulder on the pool deck where it lands with a plop. He runs the tip of a finger over my nipple, pebbled almost painfully. "You cold, Maeve?" he asks as he dips his head and takes my whole breast into his mouth. Benny knows I'm not cold, that my body is reacting to him and not the cool night air or the warm water lapping at my back with every gentle thrust.

"Nuh-uh," I murmur, locking my hands behind his head to hold him to me, hoping that he continues with his slow, sensual licks and tiny nips on my over sensitized flesh.

"This is all for me then?" He gestures at the hardened nipples he's now plucking at.

"Yessssss..." The word is torn from me as he goes back to lavishing attention on my breasts, my back arched to give him free rein.

"You like that?" he asks, his voice roughened by desire. He palms and kneads before plucking my nipple, the pleasure pain making me rock against him with more urgency. I should be embarrassed by my reaction, but I'm not. I want to come so badly, and Benny must know it because he deftly undoes the strings holding my bathing suit bottoms on, tugging it so that it slides through my pussy, touching all the parts of me that are throbbing for a release and eliciting a moan from low in my throat.

"I don't have a condom with me, Smalls, but I'm going to make you feel good, I promise." He groans against my nipple when he reaches between us to dip a finger into me. "So fucking hot and wet." Working over my clit, he slips his finger deeper this time, my position on his lap making it a little difficult. Releasing my hold on him to make it easier, I lie back, floating atop the water with my legs still locked around his waist. "Fuck, Maeve." His finger traces over the one strip of hair covering my mound. Disappearing between my folds again, he plunges into me, dragging a cry of pleasure from me. Over and over, in and out, my pleasure building higher and higher. My eyes screwed closed, my body on fire with every touch.

Without warning, he pulls me up so that we're chest to chest again, making me whimper. "I'm so close."

"I know, Smalls. Me too." This time when he rocks against me, it's not the soft cotton rubbing against my clit but the silky steel of his erection. I stiffen just slightly, but he is so in tune with my every movement that he knows. "Shhhh, I promise to keep you safe. I just want to feel you against me." I nod, knowing it to be true and wanting to feel him just as much. He drags his mouth along my jaw until his lips find mine again, his dick sliding through my slit to bump against my clit with every thrust.

"Feels so, so, so good," I purr as he increases his pace, his grip on my waist tighter, applying just the right amount of pressure.

"Fuck yeah, it does. I want you so fucking much, Smalls. I swear when I get you in a bed, it's gonna be so fucking good. I'm going to fuck every inch of you." His voice is barely audible over the sound of the water smacking against my skin and my heartbeat thundering through my ears. I had no idea until this minute that I liked dirty talk, but I do. I so do. His words have me rolling my hips at a faster pace, grinding harder, and panting with my need to come. I've never had any orgasm that wasn't self-inflicted, so I've clearly been missing out and messing around with the wrong guys. With one roll of my hips and one rock of his, I'm exploding, the stars behind my lids a meteor shower compared to the sparkles of the ones earlier. My mouth falls open as I breathlessly pant out my pleasure, my limbs as fluid as the water around us.

"Fucking fuck, Maeve." He joins me moments later, hissing my name out between his teeth, grunting as he comes. His motions slow, my head dropping to his shoulder as I take deep breaths.

After several moments, our breathing has returned to normal. Benny's hands continue to roam over the exposed skin of my back. Goose bumps erupt with every pass, and a shiver slips up my spine.

"Now you're cold." He shifts us lower in the warm water.

"Not cold, felt nice." My tongue feels thick. I'm exhausted all of a sudden, orgasms clearly take a lot out of you.

"I should be embarrassed about what just went down, Smalls, but I'm not. Not even a little." His arms come around me, swallowing my small frame, and he places kisses along my shoulder. I like this soft side of Benny. Again, he has a way of making me feel safe, protected...his.

"I'm a little embarrassed," I admit. And I am. But not because of what we did or how I reacted to his touch.

He pulls back a bit to look down at me as best as he can with me buried in his neck. "Don't be embarrassed. It was so hot. You're so hot," Benny tells me, the sincerity there in his tone.

"It was hot. But now I have to try to gracefully climb off you and figure out a way to put my suit back on. Like should you close your eyes? Look away?" I'm dead serious and legit; this is what is swirling around in my mind amid my post-orgasm glow. "And do I thank you? I should, right? I should thank you for my first real orgasm because that's a big deal. I'm totally rambling now like a crazy person."

"Whoa, whoa, whoa." Benny laughs. "Slow your roll,

Smalls. First, I am not closing my eyes or turning away. I've already seen it all, and I'm going to see it all again. Promise you that. Second, I'll get you a towel to wrap up in, and you don't even have bother with the suit," he says with the all the logic and practicality I seem to be lacking at the moment. "And what do you mean, your *first real* orgasm?" He tries again to get a look at my face, this time prying me from my hiding spot in his neck. "Please tell me you're not a virgin, Maeve." The look of fear and mild horror on his face is almost comical. "I mean, it's one thing to fuck around with you behind your brother's back, but it's another thing to fuck around with his virgin sister." With a low groan, he leans his head back against the edge of the pool.

Deciding I should put him out of his misery, I poke him in the stomach, making him curl in on himself a bit. He wasn't expecting the jab. "Now who needs to slow their roll, little drama llama?"

"Don't bring Millie into this," he mumbles, making me giggle.

"Don't worry, neither of my siblings are here, and neither are going to find out about this." I don't know what to call what we just did. I don't want to put a label on anything. "Whatever happens in Arizona stays in Arizona. We'll have our fun while we're here, then when we get home..." I trail off, not trying to ruin the moment. "And I'm not a virgin so you can stop worrying," I reassure him. His head pops up quick enough to bump mine. "Ouch."

"Sorry, Smalls." He rubs the tender spot. "So you're not a virgin?"

I shake my head, trying not to focus on the fact that he didn't agree with the whole "fun" part of our little talk.

"What did you mean then? You've smashed and not got off?" He looks stunned when I nod with a shrug of my shoulders. "Like once?"

A laugh escapes me at his incredulity, "No. Not once. I've just never had anyone able to."

"But you've had one before, right?" The concern marring his brow is touching and making this just a little less mortifying. But not by much.

"I have, but not *with* anyone." I don't know how else to say it without actually saying out loud that the only time I've ever orgasmed was from masturbating.

"Not with anyone?" He looks genuinely confused, and then he finally gets it. "Ooohhh. So you can get yourself off plenty, but the boys you've been fucking can't get the job done." He looks smug as hell right now. "Clearly, you haven't been hooking up with the right guys."

I don't like him saying that. I admitted the same thing to myself only minutes ago, but something about hearing Benny say it doesn't sit well with me. Maybe because I don't like the whole kiss and tell thing, and maybe it's that I'm not used to talking to the guy I'm with about the other guys I've been with. Benny has no limits. He's made that clear on more than one occasion. "Can we be done talking about this now?" I know that my face, neck, and chest have to be fifty shades of red right now. The feeling of heat has moved from all my happy girlie parts to my upper half and turned to embarrassment. His brow is creased again, but this time, it looks more like anger.

"Yeah, we can." Could it be that talking about me with other guys makes him mad? That should irritate me more than excite me, but I'm feeling pretty damn giddy about it. He places a kiss on my forehead and swings me off his lap and onto the ledge next to him. "Let me grab us some towels." I watch in appreciation as he pulls himself out of the pool, his muscles bunching and rippling, the water cascading over the tanned, taut skin. Unabashedly, he walks over to the towel cart and grabs one, rubbing it over his chest and head, down his torso before knotting it at his waist. The whole time, my gaze followed the path of the white cotton appreciatively. Carrying a stack of towels, he pads back my way, stopping in front of me with an outstretched hand. "Come on, Smalls. Let's get you out of there before you turn all pruney." He smiles down at me with a wicked gleam in his pretty blue eyes. There was no way he was gonna close his eyes. I can't blame him; I enjoyed the view he afforded me.

On a sigh, I take his hand, pretending to be as bold and confident as Benny is, and allow him to help me from the pool. He winks at me after his slow perusal and wraps me in the warm towel before I catch a chill. "See, that wasn't so bad." He stoops to pick up my suit and his clothes, wadding them up together before taking my hand in his and leading me to the door. "I'm not sure if your sister is still messing around with whoever is in your room, but you're staying in mine tonight."

"Benny, I cannot stay in your room!" I nearly shriek.

"Shhh, you're gonna wake people," he scolds as we make our way down the hall to the elevator. "I'll have you back to your room before practice in the morning, Maeve. I'm not nearly done with you. Especially not after that bomb you dropped on me." Benny shakes his head. "If you think I'm sending you back to your room thinking that you know what a real orgasm feels like after that half-assed shit in the pool," he says, jerking his thumb back the way we came, "you're crazy, baby."

"Benn—"

"Smalls, if you do it right, fucking is a sport, and I'm an athlete. A goddamn gold star type. That was only the first period. We still have two periods and an intermission left before the night is over." His words are punctuated with the dinging of the elevator. Hurriedly, I follow him. After that speech and his vivid analogy, I am all about letting Benny Hayes score. Repeatedly.

10

BENNY

T rue to my word, I made sure that Smalls made it to practice on time. Both of us looked a little rough from lack of sleep, but she wasn't late. Now, as I wait for the girls to come out of the locker room, I'm wondering how much sleep we would actually get if I brought Maeve back to my room for a nap. My guess is none. Not when I know what she tastes like. Can still smell her on my skin since I didn't have time to shower before the first game this morning. It was either shower and be late or go smelling like sex and Maeve Sexton. I chose the latter. I'm leaning against the wall when my phone dings with a text message. Pulling it out I curse under my breath. Levi.

> Sexy: What's up, bro? How are my sisters?

> Benny: Hey, man. They're fine

> Sexy: Heard Maeve got hurt, she good?

> Benny: Yeah, it was a nasty hit. Enforcer style!

The hit really was something right out of a hockey game.

Sexy: Damn. She's ok, though?

Benny: Yeah, Hannah's here taking care of the team. Maeve is back on the field today.

Sexy: Thatta girl. How about Millie, she giving you shit?

Benny: She tried. Maeve keeps her in line. She fucking hates me, though.

Sexy: Sounds about right. You smashing all the other softball players or what?

How do I answer that? *"Yeah bro, I'm smashing the hell out of your little sister actually."* Not sure that would go over really well.

Benny: Or what lol. Getting in a lot of ice time. I'll be ready for practice as soon as I get home.

I know changing the subject to hockey will get Levi off the topic of who I'm fucking and not fucking.

Sexy: That's what I like to hear. See you in a few.

Honestly, I feel some level of guilt, but it lasts all of three seconds and vanishes without a trace when I see Maeve coming my way, her teammates close behind. We agreed not to let them know about us either. For one, her sister would throw a damn fit, and for two, the fewer people who know, the better. This way nobody can slip in front of Levi. But not kissing the smile off her face right now might be the hardest thing I've done all day.

"Hey, girls." I say girls, but I'm looking at Maeve. Her hair is down and wavy, her nose and cheeks pink from the sun but still not able to hide her freckles. She has a pair of dark jeans on with little rips and tears giving me flashes of skin, and a black shirt that stops right at her rib cage, leaving her stomach bare.

I'm fairly certain she's trying to torture me with all this skin that I can't touch. She's usually dressed way more comfortably after her long day on the field.

"You don't have to babysit us. We're actually going out," Millie says. She, Kenna, and Lakyn are dressed a little differently than Maeve. More like they are going clubbing.

"Where you girls off to?" I ask, my brows raised in question. Again, I say girls, but I'm asking Maeve.

"Well, they're going out with Josh and some of their friends. I've decided not to go. I'm going to get a coffee and then going back to the hotel," Maeve answers, doing her best to seem nonchalant when I can see she's just as chill as I am, which is not at all.

"Are you sure you don't wanna come?" Kenna asks. "I swear I won't let that guy Shane bother you again." I let a little grunt slip out before I can stop myself. "What? I would!" she insists.

"I believe you, Ken." She wouldn't have to, though, because if Maeve decided to go out with her girls and the Delta guys, so was I.

"No. That's okay. I'm actually looking forward to just relaxing. I didn't get much sleep last night." I'm not sure if anyone else notices the blush creeping onto her face, but I do, and I'm here for it. It just tells me that Maeve is thinking about all the ways I kept her awake last night.

Millie mistakes her sister's comment as a dig on the fact that she locked her out last night to hook up with whoever she was hooking up with. "Sorry about that, sissy. Josh and I fell asleep," she says sheepishly.

"Where did you end up anyway?" Lakyn asks almost suspiciously.

I cross my arms over my chest. "Yeah, Smalls. Where did you sleep last night?" I watch her squirm a bit. She clearly hasn't thought this through. Maybe I should come to her rescue, but this is too much fun.

We're all watching her now, waiting for an answer. I am not prepared for what tumbles out of her mouth in a rushed ramble, and neither is anyone else. "I stayed with Benny in his room and let him do filthy things to me, and if any of you tell Levi, I'll never talk to you again. I mean it!" Not waiting for a response, she stalks off in the direction of the coffee shop, head held high with a swish in her hips. I can't hide the smile that slips over my lips as I watch her go. At the silence behind me, I turn to see Lakyn, Kenna, and Millie all three standing there dumbfounded. With a shrug, I set off after Maeve, thrilled not to have to pretend that's not exactly where I'm going.

"I THOUGHT for sure you would take me to play hockey," Smalls says as she places her neon pink golf ball down and lines up her shot.

"Just figured you didn't know how to play, and seriously, who doesn't love putt-putt golf?" I watch as her ball rolls down the green turf and through the windmill paddles to land on the other side near the hole.

Maeve laughs. "I've been skating since I was three and playing hockey with Levi since forever. He would tape pillows to Millie and me and put us in the goal and just shoot on us for hours and hours. It was torture, really, and probably the reason we didn't follow in his footsteps and play hockey." She leans on her club and watches as I take my turn. "Honestly, I think we broke my dad's heart a little."

My ball on the tee I mimic her stance and lean against my club, "I've seen your dad at your games and your brother's. I'm pretty sure he's not disappointed in any of you. Plus, you're a beast on the field, Smalls. If he was heartbroken even a little, he's over that shit by now." I take my shot, my ball whizzing past the moving paddle and sinking right into the cup. "Hole in one, baby. Happy Gilmore style." I walk over and pluck my ball out to make room for her to take her shot.

"Stupid hockey players. Shouldn't be allowed to play golf," she mumbles as she taps her ball and watches it fall into the hole.

When she bends to pick it up, I come up behind her as she straightens and wrap an arm around her waist. Pressing my lips to her ear with her hair tickling my face, I say, "How about loser has to go skinny-dipping tonight with the winner?"

Maeve turns her head to the side so that she can see me. Her pink lips tip up in a pretty smile. "How's that work if we're both naked? Who is the winner?"

"If you have to ask that, you must not remember how I play," I tease. My eyes focus on her mouth as I bend, kissing her pouty lips and slipping my tongue lazily against hers. And I wonder, not for the first time, how am I going to quit her when we got back home?

11

BENNY

It's past curfew, which means that the rooftop pool area is also closed for the night. I made sure to go and prop the door open earlier since they're on a timed lock. We found that out the hard way last night, but thankfully, the maintenance guy who helped us was wicked cool about it and gave me the heads-up about the automatic locks. With my backpack loaded down with extra towels, lube, a Bluetooth speaker, condoms, and anything else I could think to grab on my way out of the hotel room, I make my way to a lounger near the edge of the pool and toe off my shoes. Not wanting to unload everything, I take the speaker out and set it up, setting my Spotify app to shuffle. "Ten thirty," I murmur. Maeve said she'd be down at eleven. After we played golf, she had some team stuff to do, so I went and caught some ice time, then ran into Josh and told him to keep it in Millie's room tonight when he mentioned maybe checking out the hot tub. He nodded in understanding and said as long as he didn't have to leave till the morning that it wouldn't be a problem. I always knew that I liked him.

It's chilly again tonight as it usually is in the desert this time of year. The days are still all fucked, but the cool night makes the heated pool and hot tub even more inviting. Deciding to wait for Maeve in the warm water, I strip down to nothing, shoving the clothes in my bag, and dive in. The warm water sluices over my skin as I glide to the opposite end and then back to sit on the same ledge as last night. From here, I can't see the door, but I can see the twinkling lights of the city. It's a beautiful backdrop, the inky sky littered with a million stars seeming endless up here.

I've been in the water only about ten minutes when I hear someone making their way toward me. "You lost the bet, Smalls. Hope you're ready to pay up." I turn my head to look over my shoulder, the smile dying on my lips.

"Ooohh, can I play?"

"What the fuck are you doing here, Samantha?" I bite out in irritation. I don't know who the hell told her I was up here, but when I find out, they're catching my hands.

"I heard there was a private party up here. Am I not invited?" she says in a pouty voice, squatting down beside me making it so her dress rode up her legs high enough for me to see her underwear if I wanted to look. "A very private party I see." The pool lights do nothing to hide my nakedness and everything to highlight it.

Not wanting to engage or encourage her to stay, I look away from her and go back to looking out over the night sky. "What do you want, Sam?" I'm not sure what the hell she wants, but I need to get her out of here before Maeve shows up.

"I've been waiting for you to call me."

"I told you I wouldn't." I can see her standing out of the corner of my eye. Hopefully to leave.

"You always did like to play hard to get."

"Wasn't playing." I shake my head. "Not th—" I'm cut off by a splash in the water. What the fuck?

Breaking the surface, Samantha swims toward me in

nothing but a sheer bra and her goddamn panties. She doesn't stop until she's right in front of me, wearing a devious smile on her face. My arms are extended on either side of me on the edge of the pool, my hands flat against the decking. I refuse to cover myself. I'm not playing whatever game this is. She skims the water directly in front of me, her eyes on my flaccid cock. "I can help you with that." Even closer now, she glides into the space between my legs and goes to take me in her hand.

I catch her wrist, doing my best not to hurt her while still getting my point across. I drop it when she tugs. "Not going to happen, Samantha. Why don't you do us both a favor and stop embarrassing yourself and get out of here."

"When did you become such a prude?" she hisses out in a scathing tone.

"I'm a prude because I don't want to fuck you? Not how it works, sweetheart. I'm just not interested. Been there, done that, ya know?" My smile is condescending. I didn't want to be mean, but I'm over this bullshit. "Wasn't that great, so I moved on to better."

"Fuck you, Ben," she practically growls. Leaning into me, she does her best to press her tits into my chest as she whispers in my ear, "I was the best you ever had. You told me that yourself. Just remember that."

My laugh is as condescending as my smile. "That's because I didn't know any better. Turns out, you aren't even in the top ten."

If we weren't in the water, she would have been able to connect the slap she aimed my way, and I may have even deserved it. Again, I was able to catch her wrist before she put her hands on me. "You weren't even that good. Go fuck yourself," she says as she hauls herself out of the pool.

"I'd rather fuck myself than fuck you," I call after her retreating back, watching for as long as I can to make sure she actually leaves.

The adrenaline of the past few minutes coursing through me has me so on edge I decide to swim a few laps while I wait for Maeve. The returned peacefulness and the beauty of the night sky and the city below do nothing to help with the irritation I feel. It takes a good twenty minutes for me to find some inner peace again. Moving to the side of the pool, I pull myself out to check the time. 11:15. Maeve should have been here by now. I don't even have her number programmed in my phone to call and see where she is. How the fuck did I let that happen? Remembering that I have Kenna's number in my phone, I text her while pulling a towel around my waist

> Benny: It's Benny, you know where Maeve is?

> Kenna: I know who this is. No, haven't seen her.

> Benny: Text me her number

> Kenna: You're sleeping with her but don't have her number? Wtf!?!

> Benny: Just give it to me.

> Kenna: 555-1441

> Benny: Thanks.

Punching in her number, I wait for the ring, but instead, it goes right to voicemail. Fuck.

"Hey, Smalls. I'm at the pool. The doors open. Hopefully, you're on your way." I end the call and walk over to the door to make sure Samantha didn't lock me out, and maybe that's why Maeve isn't here. The door can't be accessed from the inside or outside without a special key card after a certain time. The door is propped open just as I left it earlier. "Where the hell is she?" I pick my way back to the chair and all my things and sit down, trying to figure out if I should wait here or go look for her. Using the towel to dry off, I start pulling my clothes out of the bag. Maeve is never late for practice—she's crazy about being on time—so something must be up. Shirt and shorts on, I slip on my shoes and gather my shit. This night turned out to be a fucking mess. I leave the pool area and head for the door, taking my makeshift stopper with me. At the elevator, I try calling Maeve once more, and once more, it goes to voicemail. "Just left the pool, going to check your room." I disconnect just as the elevator doors open. The thirty-second ride seems to take an eternity. At her door, I see the same red scarf hanging on the knob from the other night. Not giving a shit since I'm pretty certain it was Josh who told Samantha where I was, I bang on the door loud enough to wake the fucking dead. A knock the motherfucking FBI would be proud of. I'm just about to knock again when a pissed-off Millie swings the door open. How I ever worried about telling them apart, I don't know. I can tell without even trying. "Where's your sister?" I ask, not bothering with pleasantries.

"I have no idea. She had a meeting with Hanna, and she said she'd see me in the morning, so I assumed she was with you." She snarls. Like legit snarls. If she had claws, they'd be out right now.

"I haven't seen her. She was supposed to meet me and never showed."

This pleases Millie if the smile on her face is any indication. "If she didn't show, it's because she changed her mind," she says almost gleefully. "Guess you'll have to find someone else's sister to bang." Her words made definite with the slam of the door in my face.

"That went well," I mutter to myself. Maybe she went to my room. That's the only other place I can even look for her. I can't go to Hanna's room or my sister's. If Kenna doesn't know where she is, and she's not in her room or the pool, then maybe she's in my room. I gave her a key earlier this morning before practice. At my door, I wave the little card in front of the lock and wait for the light to turn green. When it does, I push open the door. "Smalls, you here?" I call into the empty room. Tossing my bag onto the neatly made bed, I flop down next to it. Where the fuck is, she? After trying one more time to call her and getting her voicemail, I put the phone on the nightstand. Pissed off that she stood me up but worried about where the fuck she is, I strip down, push the backpack on the floor, and crawl between the cool sheets. Nobody else is worried, so I guess I shouldn't be either. Easier said than done, though. She owes me a skinny-dipping pool party, and I'm for damn sure gonna call that shit in. I might collect double for making me worry.

12

MAEVE

"Hey, Smalls! What happened to you last night?"

I startle at the sound of his voice in the quiet locker room. I got here early to avoid seeing him. I should have known he would find me anyway. "Nothing happened to me. I didn't feel like swimming." I don't bother looking up from where I'm tying my cleats until I'm forced to.

He looks confused, his forehead creased, his brows angry slashes over his blue eyes. "What do you mean you didn't feel like swimming? I was there waiting for you." His tone is heavy with irritation.

"You looked like you were doing okay." I didn't mean to even tell him that I saw him, but his attitude about me not showing up is pissing me off. Who does he think he is?

"What are you talking about? So you did come to the pool, and what? You didn't feel like swimming, or you didn't feel like swimming with me?"

"I didn't feel like swimming. Not with you and not with Samantha actually"—I shrug—"so I didn't." Seeing her there with him hurt me more than I thought anything could and that scared me. I had shown up, excited that I was early. Benny was sitting on the ledge just like the night before, his arms spread wide on either side of him. I watched in appreciation as the water dripped from the long strands of his brown hair onto his broad shoulders. His tattoo, the one that I traced over and over the night before, looking distorted from the bend of his arm and the droplets of water hitting the lights. And that's when I saw *her*, Samantha. In nothing but a bra and thong, floating between his legs and whispering in his ear. The rest is a blur. Through tears in my eyes, I was able to leave as quietly as I had come in. Luckily, Hanna was just coming in from a late dinner. I stayed in her room for the night, telling her that I had gotten locked out looking for something for a headache and didn't want to wake my sister or bother anyone at the front desk to let me back into my own room. Probably not the most believable story, but I knew that he would come looking for me in my room and couldn't in hers.

Benny interrupts the memories of last night. "Me and Samantha? What in the hell are you talking about? She was in the pool for all of five minutes and then she fucked off back to her house when I told her nothing was going to happen between us. Someone told her I was on the roof, she came up there, jumped in the water, and I shot her down. Why would I be fucking around with Samantha or anyone else for that matter knowing that you were on your way up?" He shoves his hands into the pockets of his shorts, shaking his head at me. "I know I have a reputation, that all of us at Hockey House do, but still, Maeve. Have I given you any reason to think I'd do that shit to you? Have I treated you like a side piece?"

Not wanting to hear his reasoning or answer his questions, not willing to think about how sweet he's actually been to me, I plow forward as if he didn't even say anything. "Like I said, you looked like you were doing okay." I tug on the brim of my baseball cap. Even in full uniform, I feel naked standing in front of him and letting him see that I care. That I was jealous. That he...hurt me. I don't want him to see any of that. This was supposed to be just some fun. Right now, it feels anything but.

His frustration at my inability to see that what he's saying is true is apparent. "Maeve. I don't know what you think you saw, but it wasn't that. And even if it was, weren't you the one who told me that this couldn't go any further than here because Levi wouldn't like it?" He practically spits the words at me with disdain dripping from them. He likes saying them as much as he liked hearing the words the other day. They're like a thousand little daggers pinpricking my skin. Determined to make it out of here without crying, I stand straighter.

"Yup. That's what I said. I've had my fun, and now I'm done," I lie. I'm not even close to done, and I don't want to be. But he made the choice for me. I won't share, and I won't be like those girls who fall all over themselves just waiting to get whatever attention Benny or my brother or the rest of their roommates will give them. I have more self-respect than to let myself fall into that group. Those girls are looking for a story to gossip to their friends about. A ticket to the show. I'm looking for so much more.

"Just like that." It's not a question.

"Just like that." I mimic and go to walk by him and out of the locker room. It's still wicked early, and I don't have to even be on the field yet, but it's better than being in here getting my heart broken. No. Not my heart because that would mean that my heart is involved. Sure feels like my damn heart, though. Before I make it more than three steps, he hooks my arm at my elbow, stopping me in my tracks. I'm looking straight ahead at the door to freedom while his gaze burns into the side of my face. Each freckle and beauty mark feel like they're being lit on fire from the heat creeping up my neck.

"What if I'm not done?" Benny asks, his thumb sweeping over the sensitive skin at the bend of my arm. "What if this is more than just fun for me?" I shake my head. I don't need a bullshit line from him. I can't handle it. Because I want what I think he's offering, and I know I shouldn't.

He tugs on my arm, spinning me to face him. With a finger under my chin, he tilts my head back so that I'm looking at him, but the brim of my hat still blocks my eyes from his. Thankfully. I don't want him to see the tears shimmering there. My emotions are all over the place, and the tears are just one more thing for me to be mad about. I hate that they make me look weak. Benny has other ideas, though, and spins my hat around backward just like his. My shield is taken from me, and I'm forced to meet his gaze. "What if I say fuck Levi? I'll take the ass beating. I want to date you, Maeve Sexton, and I'm willing to fight your brother if that's what it takes to do it." A crooked smile softens his face that only moments ago was pulled in anger. My heart accelerates dangerously, the butterflies that had been gaining momentum since the moment he stepped into the room are now in full flight. "Not in secret and not behind anyone's back. I will go back home and walk right into my house and tell your brother that whether he likes it or not, I'm going to see where this thing between us goes." He shifts, pulling me closer to him, the clean scent of his cologne clinging to him and enveloping me. "He will undoubtedly try to kick my ass, and I will let him if it means you'll kiss me all better and nurse me back to health."

I sniffle, willing the tears clinging to my lashes not to fall. Crying when I'm mad, when I'm sad, frustrated, happy whatever has always been an irritating weakness of mine. Talk about a drama gene. Benny gently swipes them away with the back of a finger. "Don't cry. He won't *actually* kill me. He'll just hurt me a little. I promise. It'll be worth it, though." I can't help but laugh at him, glad that he doesn't seem fazed by my tears.

"Levi might kill you." I'm not entirely convinced he won't.

"He can try," Benny says, winking, his smirk reckless.

Shaking my head, I feel the anger and hurt dissipate,

knowing he wouldn't be willing to put his life, his home, and his hockey on the line if he wasn't sincere. Especially not his hockey. None of the hockey boys are about the dating life, so this is a big step for him to even admit. The realization that he has just admitted that he wants to *date* me—not just hook up whenever but *date*—is huge. I don't want to get too excited in case he was just in the moment. "You sure? I think you might have a death wish, Benny Hayes."

He pulls me flush against him now, kissing the tip of my nose. "Not a death wish, Smalls. I'm tougher than him anyway. Plus, I did win a bet, and I always collect on my bets. You owe me." His hands rest at the small of my back, fingers grazing the top of my ass.

"So what, you're gonna fight my brother over a bet then?" I toy with him, biting the inside of my cheek to keep from laughing. If you had told me just thirty minutes ago that I would be standing here, in Benny's arms, happy and hopeful, I would have called you a liar.

"Have you seen you naked? Hell yes, I'm going to fight him over a bet!" Benny's face softens. He raises his hand and traces the swath of freckles across my face from cheek to cheek. Something I've always been self-conscious of, and he has a way of making me feel beautiful *because* of them. "It's not just about the bet, Smalls. It's about you. You're the whole damn package, and if I have to play dirty to have you, then I guess I will. Isn't that what you softball girls say? Look pretty, play dirty? Well, I've got the play dirty part on lock!" His lips tilt up in that smirky smile that I can't get enough of.

Benny Hayes—funny, kind, hot as hell star forward for the FU Fire hockey team—thinks that *I'm* the whole package? I shake my head in disbelief. "Not for nothing. I mean, I don't want to ruin your badass hockey boy rep or anything, but you've got the pretty part down too." Talk about the total package.

Benny lifts me up, and I curl around him, my hands in his hair and my ankles locked at his waist. My heart feels as light as he makes the rest of me seem. "True. I'm better at the dirty part, though. Let me show you."

"Maybe I should show you." I can't contain the silly grin on my face. Instead of trying, I pull his head down for the kiss he's been teasing me with.

When he raises his chin, my sigh is audible when our lips finally meet, and he murmurs against my mouth, "Maybe you should."

EPILOGUE

Benny

With Maeve's hand in mine, I walk through the front door of Hockey House. I stop in the living room where everyone likes to hang out, today being no different. Some playing video games and others dry fucking whatever chick happened to be there today. They were always around. Some call them puck bunnies, but Millie calls them hockey hoes, and I liked that so much better.

"Where's Sexy?" I keep my voice level when I ask the room.

Murphy looks over from where he sits on the loveseat with a girl perched on his lap. His smile is wide and instantaneous until he sees Maeve tucked into my side. The grin slips from his face as his gaze travels down to where our hands are joined and then back up with a look of horror. "Oh shit," he murmurs, standing abruptly, making the girl in his lap scramble to find her footing so she doesn't land on the floor. "Everyone who doesn't live here, get the fuck out." The order startles the people in the room, but those of us who live here know what it means. It means there's about to be a fight in Hockey House, and nobody but us can be around to witness it. The coach has a strict no-fighting policy. One he takes very fucking seriously.

"Yo, Sexy! Better come down here," Cubbie yells up the stairs almost gleefully.

"Benny..." Maeve murmurs, a nervous edge in her voice.

"It's okay, Smalls." I squeeze her hand reassuringly and press a kiss to her temple. Around us, everyone is gathering their shit, not sure what's going on, sending furtive glances our way.

Just as the front door closes after the last person, I can hear footsteps on the stairs, followed by voices. Turning, I wait in the doorway for Levi to make it into the room. He comes in with Nora and her friend Jessica, pulling a shirt on over his head. Laughing at something one of them says, he slaps Jessica on the ass, making her giggle. At least he's in a good fucking mood. Maybe that will help soften the blow...to my face.

"Hi, Benny," Nora says, her voice syrupy sweet as she reaches to draw a hand down my chest. I catch her wrist before she can make contact, feeling Maeve stiffen beside me. "Goodbye, Nora," I answer, dropping her hand and looking past her.

"Yup, if you don't live here, you gotta go." Murphy lets them know, holding the door for the two girls.

"What about her?" Nora all but hisses, jerking her hand in Maeve's direction. Nora is meaner than a snake to other women. Especially if she thinks they'll get in her way and ruin her chances to ride one of our dicks to the pros. Doesn't matter whose dick, either, and we don't have a problem letting her think it'll work.

Before I can answer, Murphy slams the door in her face, turning the lock just in case.

"Hey, short stack," Levi says to his sister, grinning at her not giving a shit about Nora or her outburst. He typically doesn't pay her any attention unless she's naked.

"Hi, Le—"

Levi cuts her off abruptly. "Why are you holding my sister's hand, Benny?" He tilts his head like he's trying to piece together a puzzle and can't quite figure it out, his eyes boring into mine.

How do I say, *"Well, remember how you asked me to keep an eye on your sister? I did. And also, I've been fucking the hell out of her, and now she's my girlfriend"* to your best friend?

I'm not really sure, but I have about three seconds to figure it the fuck out. Lifting my chin, I hold his gaze, "We're dating." That was fucking lame. Way to fucking go, Hayes.

"I'm sorry, what? It sounded like you said you're dating my *little* sister," he bites out, his hands fisting at his sides.

"Levi..." Maeve starts, but again, he cuts her off. "I'm asking him, Maeve. Not you." I don't like his harsh tone. "So I ask you to keep an eye on my sisters to make sure nobody takes advantage of them, and you decided what? You might as well fuck one of them to make it worth your while?"

Maeve gasps next to me and opens her mouth to defend herself or maybe me. We knew this would go down like this, though. I raise my hand to stop her from wasting her breath. "Go over by Murph, Smalls. I've got this." I nod and push her toward him before turning back to Levi.

"Don't talk about her like that. She didn't do anything wrong. You wanna be pissed, you be pissed at me."

"Oh, don't fucking worry. I am." He laughs sardonically. "If you think for one minute I'm going to let you use my sister to get your dick wet until the next piece of ass catches your eye, you're dead fucking wrong." His breathing is unsteady, the muscle in his jaw bunched, and the vein in his temple throbbing. Levi is about three seconds from losing his fucking mind. And I can't blame him. This was never supposed to happen. But it did, and I'll be damned if I'll apologize for it.

With a shake of my head, I tell him calmly, "It's not like that, Sexy. She's not a piece—" And that's when he snaps. I don't even have time to get out of the way before he launches himself across the space separating us and swings. He lands the first punch, then the second before I get my hands up between us and push him off. I don't make it to my feet before he has me pinned to the ground again. Fucker is fast for someone so tall.

"Levi, oh mygod, stop it! You're hurting him!" I hear Maeve yell as he gets me with an elbow, making me grunt in pain. Knowing that I can't let him get too many more hits in before I'm in trouble I jerk my hips up to try to throw him off me. It works, allowing me to hop to my feet and wait for the next punch. "I gave you those for free. I deserve them. These next hits are gonna cost you, though," I warn. No way will I just let him beat my ass without fighting back.

"You're damn right you deserve them," Levi spits out. "There's a code, bro. Fucking rules of Hockey House."

"It didn't happen here, so I technically didn't break the rules." A weak attempt at twisting shit in my favor.

"It didn't have to happen here. *We* are Hockey House." Levi jerks whips his hand out to encompass the four of us.

He's right about that. We are. But rules or not, Maeve was worth it. Worth every punch her brother lands. "I'm not going to apologize, so if that's what you're waiting for, you might as well hit me again, bro." And he does.

"I'm okay, Smalls," I reassure her as she gently presses a washcloth to my busted and bleeding cheek. We're holed up in my bedroom, Murphy and Cubbie took Levi to the rink to burn off some steam since he was still mad as hell, so I wasn't worried about having her up here so soon after breaking the news to her brother.

"You shouldn't have let him hit you so many times before defending yourself," she chastises.

"I got in a couple of hits." Murphy stepped in once I started bleeding, knowing that Sexy wouldn't quit, and we wouldn't be able to hide it from Coach if it went much further.

"You should have just let me tell him."

"I'm not some pussy, Maeve. I wasn't going to hide behind my girlfriend. I knew what was going to go down here. I broke the rules. But like I told your brother, I'm not sorry. So I took the ass whooping I had coming." I shrug and pull her to stand between my legs. "Plus, now I have Nurse Maeve here to take care of me." My hands land on her waist, tugging her onto my lap to straddle my legs. "I can think of a few ways that you can make me feel better." I wink suggestively, making her laugh.

"You must have a death wish. Levi will kill you for real if he finds me in here making you "feel better."" I hear what she's saying, but she said it while rocking against me.

"First: your brother is going to be gone for hours. Second: his being here isn't going to stop me from having sex with my girlfriend, even if you are his sister." It might not win me any points with him, and it might not happen right away, but I'm doing this with Maeve. All the way.

"I'm your girlfriend?" Maeve asks, her tone soft, hopeful. I can't get enough of how sweet she is. She's all sugar and spice. The whole damn package and everything I didn't know I wanted.

"Yeah, Smalls. You're my fucking girlfriend." I pull her head down until her mouth hovers above mine. "Let me show you," I murmur against her lips, following the words with a swipe of my tongue, grinning when she sucks in a breath.

"I don't want to hurt you, Benny." She whimpers into my mouth when I roll my hips, my dick hard underneath her.

"Not gonna happen, Smalls. You're gonna ride my cock, not my face...this time." The blush that creeps across her cheeks makes me smile. She can't hide shit from me. Those pink cheeks will give her away every time. "Now strip."

I drop my hands from her waist so she can take her clothes off. When she hesitates, I reach over my shoulder and tug my shirt over my head to spur her into action. Legs spread I settle back into the loveseat I'm sitting on and watch as Maeve tosses the hoodie she had been wearing aside before shimmying out of her leggings and panties. She stands in front of me wearing nothing but that sexy blush my dirty words painted her skin with and freckles sprinkled all over her body like a pretty constellation. "Do you know how hot you are?" I ask, making her blush spread from her cheeks to her neck and across her chest.

"About as hot as Millie," she says flippantly.

Lifting my hips so I can strip off my sweatpants and boxer briefs I shake my head. "No fucking way. You are so much hotter, Smalls." I snag her wrist and pull her forward to straddle me again, groaning when her hot pussy glides over my cock.

"We're identical twins, Benny. Nobody can tell us apart," Her head falls back when I grab her hips and slide her forward and then backward, the tip of my cock bumping against her clit with each glide.

"I can tell you apart." My lips trail across her collarbone, my tongue dipping into the indentation at the base of her throat before continuing across to her shoulder.

"H-How?" she asks on a hitched breath.

"Your eyes, for one. Yours have blue flecks in them, and they change colors in the sun." I plant a kiss right on her pebbled nipple. "In the water, they're almost a clear green with a blue center." The other nipple gets the same attention. "When you come for me, the blue spreads out from the center like an explosion." I pull her closer, tighter. "That's my favorite. Why don't you show me?" My hands palm her ass, squeezing as I watch my cock slip through her pussy, wet from how soaked she is.

"I need you inside, Benny. I'll show you anything you want. Please."

She doesn't have to ask me twice. I wrap my arms around her and bend us so that I can reach my wallet on the floor. Snagging a condom, I raise us back to a sitting position, making her laugh. "That's one way to get a workout."

"I'm about to show you another way, my favorite way," I tease. Tearing open the condom, I hand it to her, watching as she rolls it on. Not wanting to wait another second to be inside her, I wrap an arm around her waist, pulling her up onto her knees, my mouth finding hers as I grab my cock at the base and ease her onto it.

"Ohhhh, Benny." She moans, her hands burrowing into my hair, nails raking against my scalp. "Don't move, give me one second. Mmm." I give her time to adjust to my size. Her pussy is so fucking tight, I'm fighting coming already. I haven't asked her body count, but the vise grip she has on my cock makes me believe it's low as hell. Not wanting to hurt her but needing to move, I roll my hips gently, wrapping my hand in her loose hair, tugging to expose her neck. My tongue lands on her pulse point, sucking and biting on her skin without caring if I leave marks on her.

"You good, Smalls?" Fuck, I hope so. I need...more.

"Mm-hmm. I'm ready now. You're so big."

I chuckle. "You're a real sweet talker, ya know that?" One hand buried in her hair the other wrapped around her, smashing her perfect tits against my chest, I surge up, hitting bottom and making her scream out.

"Oh, god. Do that again," she pleads. Releasing my hold on her hair just enough so that I can see her face, I do it again, grinding at the end and moaning when the walls of her pussy clench me even tighter. She whimpers, "Again."

"You gonna come, Smalls?" I plunge deeper, making her moan. "Open your eyes, show me. Let me see you when you come apart all over my cock." Eyes on me she rocks against me, riding me, gaze locked on mine, arms wrapped around my shoulders. My jaw is clenched so tight, my molars gnashed together trying to hold off from coming. I've never in my life been ready to blow this soon, but the minute I slid into Maeve, I was fighting it. "That's it, so fucking tight. Pussy so good." I ramble off words, nonsensical shit between thrusts. When her eyes start to close, I slap her ass. "Don't you dare, Smalls. I wanna see that blue in your eyes explode when you do."

"I'm so close. So, so close." Her impossibly tight pussy gets even tighter.

"Yeah?" Not sure if I'll be able to hold back, I reach between us and pinch her clit gently just like she likes. Rolling it in time with the rhythm of her hips. "I'm going to come with you, Maeve. I can't help it. You drive me fucking crazy. This pussy, it's just..." I thrust into her, deep and hard, my fingers still pulling at her clit. "So. Fucking. Good."

"Benny, Benny, Benny," she chants, pressing down as I drive up. Once more and there it is. The blue in her eyes explodes like a super nova at the same time she does. Maeve's pussy pulses around me almost painfully. My name falling from her lips has me coming right after her, chasing her orgasm with my own.

"Fucking, fuck, Smalls," I grit out between my clenched teeth as wave after wave of pleasure rolls over me, my come being milked from me by her perfect pussy until a shuddering groan leaves me, and I fall back against the loveseat, spent like I just played a game that went into double overtime. It was that intense. A tremble rips through her body, tiny in my arms. A shaky breath leaves her lips as she rests her forehead to mine, my hands traveling over her. Any place I can reach, up and over, tracing over freckles, skating up the line of her spine, the curve of her hip, the dips above her ass. Over and over helping to bring us down from the high we were just riding. I can't help but be a little embarrassed. "I'll make that up to you as soon as I catch my breath," I promise.

Maeve sits back and looks at me, confusion pinching her brow. "Make what up to me? That was incredible."

"You and this magical pussy turned me into a two-pump chump."

She bursts into laughter, slapping my chest. "You're so ridiculous."

"Ridiculous or not it's true. I'm just glad I got to see your eyes do their thing." I smile and run my thumb over her bottom lip. "Hottest Sexton twin in all the fucking land."

Her skin is already flushed, but still, the blush creeps across her cheeks. "Tell me how else you can tell us apart," she says as she mindlessly traces the lines of my tattoo, and that's all it takes for me to get hard again.

I stand with her in my arms, her legs automatically wrapping around my waist, and walk us over to the bed. "Why don't I show you?"

The End

FU HOCKEY SERIES

You can meet the Fulton University Fire hockey and softball teams in the following books. They can be read as complete standalones but are more enjoyable if they're read in order. You can find them all on my website here.

Sin Bin
Arena Lights
Sweater Weather

Keep reading for a sneak peek of Sweater Weather ...

SWEATER WEATHER: CHAPTER ONE

Chapter One
Levi

Bodies. Wall-to-wall bodies. Writhing. Grinding. Leaning. Dancing bodies. Some in way fewer clothes than Boston in January calls for, but I am in no way complaining.

With a drink in hand, I make my way through the crowd to my kitchen.

"Yo, Sexton! What's up, my man?" Murphy James—my friend, roommate, and the best damn goalie in the league—greets me. "You see your sisters and their friends?" He bites down on one of his knuckles. Homeboy has it bad for my little sister's best friend. As long as it's not Millie, I'll let him live. I'm already down one roommate who thought it would be cool to date one of my sisters. I can't handle any more of that shit right now.

"No. What the fuck are they even doing here? You invite them, or did Benny?"

The guilty-as-hell look on his face gives me my answer. "I might have told them they could come if they brought Raegan."

He shrugs. "Figured Benny would have told Maeve anyway, though," Murph says, referring to our traitor roommate and my other sister.

"And did they?" I question. Shaking my head at his dumb ass and trying not to growl at the mention of Benny Hayes and Maeve. Clearly still a wicked-sensitive topic with me.

"Oh yeah. And some other chick. Wicked hot, bro. Never seen her before. Cubbie called dibs," Murphy tells me with a grin, knowing damn well that I don't give a fuck what Cubbie calls.

Topping off my *drink*—juice since I gotta be on the ice early —I slap him on the back and go to find my sisters. I know they're safer here in Hockey House than anywhere else on campus, but still. You put a bunch of drunk college boys together, then throw in a set of twins, and you're asking for fucking trouble. Shit goes down at these parties that I like to pretend my little sisters don't know about, let alone participate in. Definitely shit I don't want them to see *me* participating in.

I catch a flash of red hair in the sea of people in the living room and weave my way in that direction. Stopping to say hi to people along the way. Some with high-fives and a clap on the back, others with a wink and a slap on the ass. I need to find my sisters and get them out of here. I'm catching serious fuck-me eyes from Nora and her friend. Can't for the life of me remember her name, but I do remember that she sucks dick like a porn star and that she and Nora are always up for a good time. With that in mind, I point at the ceiling and the bedrooms up there and mouth to Nora, "Later." I grin when she nods her head. Yeah, my sisters need to go. I don't care what Benny says. He can go with them.

After a few more minutes of searching and stopping, I finally find them in the yard by the bonfire, making their red hair look like it's literally on fire. Coming up behind the pair, I tug on Millie's ponytail, only knowing it's her and not Maeve by the number ten on the back of her Fulton University hoodie. The twins are identical. I'm not even sure my mother can tell them apart. Mill whirls around, ready to fight until she sees it's me.

"Levi, you punk! I almost hit you," she says, shoving my shoulder.

"Wouldn't have hurt, short stack," I tease before going all serious older brother. "What are you doing here? Does Dad know?"

"Hi, Levi," Maeve says sweetly, squeezing me around the waist. Maeve is sugar, all sweet and pure, whereas Millie is cayenne pepper and just this side of evil, always getting them into some kind of trouble.

"Hey, Maevey. Dad and Mom know you're here?" I question since the evil twin isn't answering.

Plucking the red Solo cup out of Millie's hand, I bring it to my lips for a sip to make sure it's not alcohol. She flips me off when I hand it back to her, satisfied that it's the same juice I've been drinking.

"Just checking, Mill, can't have any underage drinking here." That earns an epic eye roll, but I don't care. They won't be drinking here or anywhere else on campus. They're nineteen, which doesn't really matter in college, but it sure as fuck does when you have an older brother at the same school.

"Daddy knows we're here. He said we could come, but when you said it was time, we had to go straight home."

Millie rolls her eyes again. "Dad wanted me to remind you to be in his office at six."

"Yeah, I'll be there." I nudge Maeve. "Where's your boy? He not showing his face because I blacked his eye?" I ask smugly. To say I didn't take it well when I found out my friend and roommate was dating my sister is the understatement of the fucking year. He had it coming, though, and he knew it. He broke rule one of Hockey House, Thou shall not fuck with the

Sexton twins. I'm the only one of the roommates with sisters, so that rule was sacred and taken seriously until Benny got my sister in a different state and away from my watchful eye. Fucker. I asked him to keep an eye on them. He took it a little too fucking seriously.

"He's not hiding, you bully. He's at the Pro Shop working for another hour. I told him I'd wait here," Maeve tells me.

I nod and am just about to ask if they know what Dad wants when Raegan walks up with some smokin' hot chick I've never seen before. Must be the new girl. Her gaze lands on mine. Bored gray eyes take me in for a moment, giving me time to do the same to her. She's a little shorter than the twins, way shorter than Rae, who towers over her, probably five-four at the most. Her honey-colored hair is tied back with a black ribbon, giving her a sexy schoolgirl vibe. She's dressed casually, more like my sisters and less like most of the girls here. Her jeans have holes in the knees, and she has a long-sleeved Tennessee Arrows shirt on, the number eight etched right above her heart, teasing over an awesome rack. Girl's got curves for days. "Oh my god, Becky," I mumble under my breath as my gaze lands on her rounded hips, and I catch a glimpse of a perfect bubble ass when I crane my neck a bit to see around her.

There's a chorus of throat clearing that finally has me bringing my eyes back up to her face. An eyebrow raised, a look of utter disgust on her face, her nose crinkled with it making me notice the light splash of freckles there and across her cheeks. Somehow, they don't make her look like a toddler, the way I swear my sisters' freckles make them look. No, these are sexy. Adding to that schoolgirl thing.

"You're new," I say, ignoring my sisters shaking their heads at me from behind her. They obviously appreciated me checking out their friend as much as she did.

"And you're an asshole," the new girl with the killer rack spits out, calling my attention to her full lips and the beauty mark above her mouth, Marilyn Monroe style. She's a fucking smoke show.

"Nah, not an asshole, doll. Just a guy who appreciates great tits and a stellar ass." I smirk, enjoying it way too much that I'm pissing her off.

"Oh my god, Levi!" Maeve admonishes.

"Saffie, I am so sorry. My brother usually saves his disgustingness for when we're not around and definitely for his skanks and not our friends," Millie explains, glaring at me. I can feel it. I've still not looked away from their stupidly hot friend, the one who's still shooting daggers at me.

"Saffron Briggs, meet my dumbass brother, Levi Sexton."

That caused her to break eye contact long enough to roll her eyes. "Let me guess, you're 'Sexy Sexton.' The one I've unfortunately *heard* about?" My sisters make gagging noises. They hate that nickname and the stories that go with it. But the way she says it in that hot little Yankee clip she has going on, definitely not from Massachusetts, has me forgetting all about the pain-in-the-ass twins and thinking way too much about their friend and what kind of things I'd like to do to her.

I shrug and tuck my hands in the pockets of my sweats. "So you've heard about me, then? Want me to show you how I got that nickname?" I offer, goading her.

She scoffs and then smiles sweetly. "No thanks. You're not my type."

With raised eyebrows, I nod in understanding. "Ooooh, you're a lesbian. That's cool. I'm all about one love, bi-love, self-love. Whatever." I grin, flashing my dimples in added innocence, letting her know that her ice-queen bitchy attitude doesn't faze me.

"Oh, I like boys just fine. And even girls occasionally. It's you I don't like," she retorts smugly. "Plus, I have a boyfriend." I watch as she pulls a chain from the collar of her shirt, a massive ring hanging from it.

"Is that a high school ring?" I ask, just barely holding back my laughter. She's cute when she's pissed, and her boyfriend is clearly lame as fuck. "Do guys still do that?"

Her glare is enough to light my ass on fire right where I stand, but I don't care. I don't care about the tool boyfriend, either. If I want her, the boyfriend is her problem, not mine. And Cubbie can fuck off calling dibs.

Murphy comes up just then, slapping me on the back, drawing my attention. He greets my sisters using their hated nickname. "Hey, Off-limits, you two behaving?

They give him a double eye roll and laugh him off. "Raegan, how about you? You being a good girl?"

Blushing at him, she just nods. Rae *is* a good girl. She's been my sister's best friend since they were tiny kids and a constant in my home. Aside from her pink hair and being so tall, she and the twins might as well be triplets. They've been attached at the hip since kindergarten.

"Good, good." Murph booms before turning to Saffron-Saffie, as my sister called her, who still has me locked in an epic *I hate your guts but refuse to look away first* stare down.

"Who's your new friend, Sexy? She looks like she really likes you," he says, laughing.

"That's enough, you guys. Leave her alone," Millie snaps. "She's Raegan's cousin, her name is Saffie, she has a boyfriend, and you can go now." My sister dismisses and waves us off.

I bark out a laugh. "Cool it, short stack. Saffie can take care of herself. I'm not gonna bite. Much," I add, snapping my teeth at her and then grinning when she rolls her eyes at me again. Between the three of them, their eyes are gonna fall right out of their damn heads from all the rolling they've been doing.

Murphy chooses that moment to say, "Speaking of biting, Nora and her friend Ava are looking for you. I'll keep an eye on these four."

I bet he will. Actually, he, Cubbie, and Benny, even if he is on my shit list, are the only guys on campus I would ever trust with my sisters. Not because they have some stellar reputation or anything. They're not even close to being fucking saints, but they do have mad respect for me, and that carries over to Millie and Maeve. Benny may have fucked up, but I would've done more than blacked his eye if I didn't think he had good intentions regarding Maeve. It would have been the last time he looked at my sister, let alone dated her.

"Ladies, behave please and remember not to take drinks from anyone you don't know and to kick anyone getting handsy right in the fucking balls. That goes for your little boyfriend, too," I order, pointing a finger back and forth between them. My sisters and Raegan promise. Saffie doesn't say a thing. I wave and leave them with Murph, then go in search of Nora and her porn star friend. It'll take the two of them to get my mind off the new girl. Saffron Briggs. Even her name is hot.

About an hour has passed, and we still haven't made it upstairs to my room because Nora wants to wait for another friend of theirs who is "just *dying* to meet me." Who am I to deny her?

Kicked back in my oversized chair, Nora is tucked into my side, kissing my neck, while Ava, with her back to me, grinds against my cock to the beat of the music booming loudly from our makeshift DJ. She could teach a thing or two to some strippers I've seen. I let my head fall back and allow my mind to shut down and my body to just feel. The minute my eyes drift closed, a wicked-hot blond with flashing gray eyes and a smart mouth appears behind my lids. I groan. Fucking hell. Fighting with Saffie was hot. I'm so used to sorority chicks and puck bunnies just looking to score a hockey player that a little hard to get might be fun. Not that I don't love easy, because I do. But a little game of chase me is something I can get down with.

My eyes pop open when I hear a snort to find the gray eyes I had just been thinking about glaring first at me, then flicking to the girls draped all across my lap.

I smirk at her anger. Why she's pissed, I don't know. Dimples flashing, I wink at her before closing my eyes again. Oh yeah. She's gonna be fun.

To see what happens between Levi and Saffron, grab Sweater Weather now.

ABOUT THE AUTHOR

USA Today Bestselling author, Mandi Beck has been an avid reader all of her life. A deep love for books always had her jotting down little stories on napkins, notebooks, and her hand. As an adult she was further submerged into the book world through book clubs and the epicness of social media. It was then that she graduated to writing her stories on her phone and then finally on a proper computer.

A wife, mother to two rambunctious and somewhat rotten boys, and stepmom to two great girls away at college, she shares her time with her husband in Chicago where she was born and raised. Mandi is a diehard hockey fan and blames the Blackhawks when her deadlines are not met. Ask her who her favorite hockey player is though, and she'll tell you that he calls her...mom.

You can find all of her books and sign up for her newsletter on her website.